PIPPA PARK
RAISES HER GAME

PIPPA PARK
RAISES HER GAME

Erin Yun

Fabled Films Press
New York

For information address Fabled Films LLC, 200 Park Avenue South, New York, NY 10003.
info@fabledfilms.com

Published by Fabled Films LLC, New York

ISBN: 978-1-944020-28-6
Library of Congress Control Number: 2019939139

Fifth Edition: November 2022

5 7 9 11 12 10 8 6
Cover Designed by Jaime Mendola-Hobbie & George McKeon
Jacket Art by Bev Johnson
Interior Book Design by Notion Studio
Text set in Zilla Slab
Printed by Everbest in China

FABLED FILMS PRESS
NEW YORK CITY
fabledfilms.com

For information on bulk purchases for promotional use, please contact the Fabled Films Press Sales department at info@fabledfilms.com

"That was a memorable day to me, for it made great changes in me. But it is the same with any life."

—Charles Dickens, *Great Expectations*

To those who opened this book:
I am happy you are here.

1

THE STRANGE ENCOUNTER

I was the only person in the park.

Tucking a damp strand of hair back behind one ear, I surveyed the abandoned slides and empty benches. It was just past six p.m. on a Friday, but it looked like nobody else wanted to be out in the rain. As I strode briskly forward, icy wind numbed the tips of my fingers, making me clutch my basketball tighter. Even though we hadn't officially left summer behind, the cold front that had settled over Victoria, Massachusetts, didn't show any signs of leaving.

So . . . empty court. Lousy weather. And things at home were just as dismal.

My older sister, Mina, had just grilled me for nearly an hour after finding out about the "unacceptable" grade I had received on my latest algebra quiz. When she finally finished, I stormed out of the apartment, making sure to grab my basketball and a water bottle; I planned on being gone awhile.

Now I kind of wished that I had taken a warmer jacket, too. Or at least a hat. But rain or shine, I wasn't ready to go home yet.

I headed past the playground equipment, where the swings swayed back and forth, their rusted metal chain-links creaking in the wind, a chilling noise that made me look twice over my shoulder as I passed them. The basketball court was just up ahead, hemmed in by the line of dense trees that marked the start of Grey Woods. The woods were named for some rich guy who had given the land to the town back in the last century, but on a day like today the name was eerily appropriate. In the drizzle and fog, the shadowy, thick trunks made me uneasy.

Rotating the ball between my stiff, raw hands, I stepped onto the centerline. I inhaled deeply and felt my back muscles start to relax. Basketball did that for me every time. I dribbled my ball toward the hoop. As I concentrated on the way the ball felt bouncing against the tips of my fingers, thoughts of impossible algebra problems and my nagging sister faded from my mind. Every movement felt natural, like the ball wasn't something outside my body but a part of it.

I headed to the free-throw line, dribbled twice, and sent the ball arcing toward the hoop. *Swish*. Nothing but net. It was one of the most satisfying things in the world to watch the ball whoosh through that hoop—and, not to brag or anything, but I was good at it. Actually, I was more than good; I was great.

Which was why I needed to get back on the school team. I had managed to make it on my first try—a big deal for a sixth grader—and by the end of last year, I'd been on the starting lineup for every game. My plan for this year had been to become the team's star player. But that dream had died quickly after my math grades dipped last spring, and Mina barred me from rejoining the team.

Her husband, Jung-Hwa, had gently tried to talk her out of it—but Mina nearly bit his head off. The best I could do was get her to agree that if I got better grades this year, she'd think about it. But a D on my first quiz today had sealed my fate.

Swish, swish, swish.

Not to mention, she had Omma on her side. That's my mom, Ji-Min. Although I had been born in the U.S., my mom wasn't a citizen, and she hadn't been able to renew her work visa when it expired around my fifth birthday. So she'd left me here with my sister and Jung-Hwa. But even though she lives back in South Korea, Omma still rules my life with her strong Korean fist. When Mina tells her about my latest scholastic failure, I'll definitely get a brutal lecture. No distance, not even 7,000 miles, can make Omma any less intimidating.

At the thought of that phone call, my concentration broke, and the ball rebounded off the edge of the rim at a wild angle and bounced into the woods. There went my streak.

With a sigh, I peered into the darkening trees. The rain clouds made it hard to tell how late it was, but I thought I must have been playing for at least an hour.

A gust of wind swept across the desolate court and whipped at the swings, which began screeching once again. I frowned; I should call Mina. I had left without telling her where I was going or when I'd be back, and that was never a good thing, especially when she was already mad at me.

I reached into my left pocket for my phone, but it wasn't there. It wasn't in my right one either. Of course. In storming out, I had forgotten to bring it. What else could go wrong? I took a long swig from my water bottle then set it down and headed after my ball.

I jogged across the court, but at the edge of the woods I skidded to a stop. A tall, hooded figure lurked among the trees.

The stranger took a step toward me. And then another. And another. My mouth opened and I felt a scream welling up, but all that came out was a little squeak.

People always say that in situations of high stress, you're supposed to have a fight-or-flight reaction. Not me. The stranger came closer but instead of sprinting in the opposite direction, I froze. Apparently, in addition to struggling with algebra, I was also screwing up the "stranger danger" lessons Mina had been drilling into my head since kindergarten.

There was a state prison right outside town . . . what if this was an escaped convict? A murderer? Was I going to be the next victim of an escaped convict murderer?

The man's forest-green hoodie shadowed his face. He held my basketball in one hand and a bulky black case— narrow at the front and wider at the back—in the other. What did he have stashed in the case? The remains of his last victim?

"Please don't hurt me," I blurted out. "Mina would kill me if I, well, died."

The stranger stopped short. And then, with an annoyed *huff*, he held out my ball to me. That's when I realized that the mysterious figure was a teenage boy—and probably too young to be a seasoned killer. Underneath the green hoodie, there was a slight roundness to his acne-scarred face that made me think he couldn't be older than seventeen.

"Take your basketball," he commanded as he set the black case on the ground. His voice sounded a little froggy, like he had a cold.

For the first time, we locked eyes. By this point, my vision had adjusted to the dark, and I could see that his eyes were an intense hazel shade.

"Thank you," I said automatically. Mina had always taught me to say please and thank you, and although I wasn't sure what the rules on politeness were regarding mysterious strangers, some habits were hard to shake. Still slightly wary,

I took the ball and clutched it against my ribcage.

Meanwhile, now that his hands were free, Green Hoodie jammed one of them into the pocket of his jeans. What was he reaching for? I leaped back.

He gave me a sour look as he pulled out . . . a cell phone. I started to breathe normally again.

"You play for one of the middle schools around here?" he asked.

"I used to. For Victoria Middle. My sister made me quit because of my grades."

The words were out before I could stop myself. Why was I even talking to him?

"That's a shame. You're good."

"Do you play basketball?"

What was wrong with me? Now I was the one keeping the conversation going.

Instead of answering, Green Hoodie scowled down at his phone and gave it a little shake. He patted his pockets. Wrinkled his nose.

"You don't happen to have a portable charger on you, or something?"

I riffled through my pockets even though I one hundred percent knew I did not have a portable charger on me; I didn't even own one. I did, however, discover a crinkled packet containing one semi-squished Happy Promise Custard Cake. I looked at the packet and then, for some reason, I handed it to him. It was not remotely close to what he had asked for, but I guess I thought he looked hungry. Or maybe just sad.

"No charger, but I have this," I said. "It's a Korean snack. From Lotte—the best brand. They're really good."

Green Hoodie stared at me, then at the Happy Promise Custard Cake, then back to me again. He pressed his lips together like he was suppressing a frown. Or maybe he was contemplating killing me after all. I gulped.

But then his lips softened into a smile. "Thank you," he said, taking the cake. He paused, and then said it again. "Thank you . . . er, what's your name?"

"Oh. Pippa. Pippa Park."

Oh man! I definitely wasn't supposed to tell him my name. I wanted to hit my palm against my forehead. Idiot!

He squinted as a pair of headlights lit up the street outside the court. He took a step back toward the woods, and his eyes darted in every direction. "If anyone asks, I was never here, okay?"

All right, now that was definitely sketchy.

"Not a problem," I said, "since I don't even know who you—"

"Thanks, Pippa. Pippa Park."

With that, he disappeared. And I was back to standing in an empty park—still cold, still damp, still alone, and now bewildered as well. For a minute, I stared into the woods, replaying our conversation in my mind and wondering where he was going with his black case in this chilly rain. Then the drizzle began to turn into a heavier rain, and thunder rumbled. I shook myself. What was I doing? What time was it? Mina was going to kill me!

Inhaling sharply, I clutched my basketball and started jogging home. As my sneakers thudded across the damp pavement, I pushed any lingering thoughts of Green Hoodie from my mind.

After all, it wasn't like I would ever see that guy again.

2

MEET THE SIBLINGS

By the time I reached my block, I was panting and thoroughly drenched. I slowed to a quick walk, attempting to catch my breath. I peered up through the rain at the blocky apartment buildings on my street. To anyone but those of us who lived around here, they all looked identical: five-stories high with gray brick and cherry-red doors that shed paint chips onto the sidewalk. But to me, it was easy to spot the details that breathed life into the neighborhood, from the Lees' billowing laundry, perpetually left out to dry on the fire escape (and now totally soaked), to the Flynns' Christmas lights blinking in the window all year long, to the collection of potted aloe vera plants on Mrs. Wilson's windowsill. Mrs. Wilson claimed the light-green sap could heal anything from bruises to sunburns to acne.

I turned the corner of my street and passed by the

Lucky Laundromat. It was a small but tidy place, with its name painted on the window in pastel blue. Mina had opened it nearly eight years ago, and while business wasn't booming by anyone's standards, it kept us afloat, alongside Jung-Hwa's long hours working at a computer-chip manufacturing company. My mom sent what she could from Korea, but she'd had to switch to part-time work because of some health problems, so it wasn't much.

As I hurried upstairs to face Mina, I prayed for my own kind of luck—that she would let me go to my room without another lecture. I reached our apartment on the second floor, and hesitated. Gathering my courage, I twisted my long, dark hair to squeeze out some of the rainwater and then, trying to be as quiet as possible, I inserted my key into the lock and nudged the door open.

It smelled faintly of sour *kimchi* and salted mackerel, but I couldn't hear anyone moving in the kitchen, and the cramped entry hall was mercifully empty. I heard the faint sounds of a TV coming from Mina and Jung-Hwa's bedroom, making my heartbeat speed up with hope. Maybe Mina was absorbed in one of her favorite, cheesy K-dramas.

I slipped off my shoes and started forward—but I hadn't gotten more than a few steps when Mina's voice startled me.

"Do you know how worried we were?"

I hugged my basketball tighter against my chest as my older sister came storming out of her bedroom. She stopped a few feet in front of me, indomitable, her dark eyes narrowed and her clenched fists resting on her hips. Behind her, Jung-Hwa ran a big, calloused hand through his shaggy dark hair and hunched his broad shoulders. He looked worried—but I suspected it had more to do with Mina than with me. When my sister was angry, everyone suffered.

"I was just in the park," I replied. "I lost track of time." I thought briefly of the guy in the woods, but I didn't say anything about him. Partly because he had told me not to, but also because it would only have complicated things. "And I would have called, but—"

"But you left your phone at home," Mina finished. She held up my battered cell. "Again." I made a grab for it, but she pocketed it before I could reach it. "This chunk of plastic could pay groceries for a month, not that it matters to you."

"Come on, *yeobo*," Jung-Hwa said, reaching forward to massage the back of Mina's neck. But not even the cutesy endearment could calm my older sister. She shook off Jung-Hwa's hand and stepped closer to me.

"You know, if you spent half the time on your schoolwork that you do dribbling that stupid thing around—"

"It's called a basketball," I interrupted her tirade.

"I don't care what it's called!"

"Well, maybe that's the problem," I said hotly. "You never care!"

"Did you hear that, Jung-Hwa?" Mina laughed without humor. "I never care."

Jung-Hwa's shoulders slumped some more. He hated when we fought, but we both knew it would only make things worse if he stepped in.

"Who cooks your meals?" Mina ranted. "Who cleans your clothes? Who pays for that basketball and this phone? Me! I brought you up by hand, all on my own! Although right about now, I have half a mind to really bring you up by hand. . . . " The tips of Mina's fingers twitched, like she was thinking about giving me a good slap. "How much more care do you need? You live in my home. Eat my food. I raised you as if you were my own child—"

"But I'm not your child!" I snapped. "And you're not my mom, no matter how much you act like it!"

"Yeah? Well, I'm glad I'm not Omma! Because then I'd have a disappointment for a daughter!" Mina stepped closer to me. "Omma left you behind so you could grow up here, in America. She gave up everything for you, but you don't appreciate anything."

Tears welled up in my eyes. Quickly, I pinched the piece of skin between my thumb and pointer finger as hard as I could. I'd read somewhere online it was supposed to stop you from crying, but the first couple of tears slipped down my cheeks anyway.

The thing was, Mina was right, and that's what hurt most. It would crush Omma to know that despite her sacrifices, I could barely pass math.

"Don't do that." At the sight of my tears, Mina cleared her throat and crossed her arms, the closest to an apology I would get. She went on, her voice somewhat gentler. "I'm serious about your grades, Pippa. I know you're young, but you have got to start taking your schooling seriously."

Toward the end of the sentence, Mina's voice started to rise again. She pursed her lips and inhaled sharply. Jung-Hwa nodded encouragingly at this. He was always trying to make Mina inhale through the nose and exhale through the mouth for five seconds whenever she felt herself getting heated.

Mina exhaled. "I did some research," she said. "The Lakeview School has a free tutoring program, and I've signed you up. From now on, you're going to be spending your Tuesday evenings studying math."

"What? I didn't agree to that!" I protested, wiping away a stray tear with the back of my hand. No way was I going to get tutored by one of those horrible, conceited private school kids. Wasn't cruel and unusual punishment illegal?

"I don't need your permission, Pippa. But I would like

your cooperation, and if you want *this* back—" Mina held up my phone— "then you'll do as I say."

Before I could continue the fight, Jung-Hwa cleared his throat and stepped in between us. His good-natured face was scrunched up in an anxious smile.

"I think everyone is pretty tired right now," he said. "Why don't we discuss the tutor later?"

"What's there to discuss?" I snapped. "It's not like I get a choice."

I stomped past Jung-Hwa, grabbed my cell phone from Mina, and stormed into my room. I knew Mina, and when she acted like this there was no changing her mind.

For a long while afterward, I could hear the low voices of Mina and Jung-Hwa in the living room. When Jung-Hwa's heavy footsteps headed toward my door a half hour later, I quickly shut off the lights and dove under the covers, burying my head in my pillow.

My door creaked open.

"Pippa? You awake?"

I didn't answer.

Jung-Hwa crossed over to me and ruffled my hair. "Don't take your sister's words too hard," he whispered. "She just wants the best for you."

He took my hand, unfurled my clenched fist, and placed something papery and thin in my palm. "Don't tell your sister."

In the dim light streaming in from the hallway, I could see a crumpled five. When I glanced up, his face looked hopeful.

"Just a little pocket change so you can pick up something sweet," he said. "Like some Choco Pies. Or maybe those walnut cakes filled with red bean paste? You used to love those. Whenever Mina would buy them, she would have to hide the package, or you'd finish the whole thing before the rest of us could try one. Remember? She hid those cakes inside cereal boxes, kitchen drawers, empty shoeboxes. You name it." Jung-Hwa laughed. "But you'd always find them."

I forced a chuckle. Jung-Hwa tapped me on my nose—a tiny gesture that he had been doing once a day for as long as I could remember—and then headed to the door.

As he closed it, I sighed under my breath. I loved Jung-Hwa. My own father had died less than a year after I was born, but Jung-Hwa tried hard to fill that role for me. He was the kind of person who was happy if the people around him were happy, and the kind of person who would take the blame if, er, *someone* happened to accidentally turn all of Mina's white underwear pink.

But he was also the kind of person who thought that an extra helping of dessert made everything okay.

I felt bad the moment that thought went through my mind. Jung-Hwa tried his best. But despite his good intentions, my future still looked abysmal. No more basketball team, and now tutoring once a week with a snobby Lakeview kid.

Sorry, but no amount of Choco Pies or walnut cakes could fix this.

3

THE HAVERFORD HOME

On Tuesday, I trudged into math and took my usual seat next to my closest friend, Buddy Johnson.

"You look miserable," he observed.

I shot him a sour look. "Gee, thanks."

I'd met Buddy back in the third grade, when he had moved to Victoria all the way from Alabama. The day Maximillian Graver, the class bully, had stolen Buddy's cookies from his lunch bag, I shared my buttery waffle snacks with him and gave him hope for the future. The look on his face—tears rolling down his pudgy cheeks even as he stuffed waffle after waffle into his mouth—had cemented our friendship. He'd grown out of the pudgy cheeks, but we'd been close ever since. Close enough for him to get away with calling me miserable looking, even.

I scowled, thinking about the reason behind my unhappiness—my first tutoring session was today. With a sigh, I crossed my legs, and a stickiness under my right sneaker captured my attention. I'd stepped in chewed gum in the hallway. Again. I peered at the underside of my shoe with disgust.

"Is that the second time, or the third?" Buddy's brown eyes sparkled with amusement. "Come on, Park, we've only been back for two weeks."

He stretched his gangly legs out in front of him and admired his battered basketball shoes. Before I could reply, our teacher, Mr. Raskol, hurried through the door. He was one of the tallest men I had ever seen—practically seven feet. He would have made a great basketball center—if he'd been the type to enjoy team play. Unfortunately for those of us in his class, Mr. Raskol seemed a lot more comfortable grading tests than interacting with actual humans.

"Settle down, everyone," he boomed, as he always did. "Everyone pass the homework up, and let's flip to page forty-two in the textbook."

I turned to the correct page and peered down at the strings of letters and numbers, gnawing the inside of my cheek as I tried to make sense of them. *Tried* being the key word.

"Would anyone like to volunteer to answer this first question?" Mr. Raskol peered around the room.

Not me, not me. I stared down at my desk, banking on the ridiculous notion that if I couldn't see him, he couldn't see me, either.

"What about . . . you, Ms. Park?"

At the sound of my name, I cringed. Did I look like I was volunteering?

Mr. Raskol pointed to the chalkboard, where an equation loomed: *If* 7 + 2x = 3x-1, *then what is x?*

I swallowed. Numbers alone were bad enough. What masochist had decided to throw the alphabet in as well?

Everyone waited. I stared at the board. Everyone waited some more.

Behind me, someone hissed, "Aren't Asians supposed to be good at math?" A quiet snicker followed.

I scowled.

Stereotypes sucked, but sometimes not being able to live up to the stereotype felt even worse. I tugged nervously at my hair, wishing I could hide behind it.

Buddy kicked my chair, and I gave him a quick glance. *Eight*, he mouthed.

I dutifully repeated the number out loud.

"Thank you, Buddy," Mr. Raskol said, making both of us flush.

With a long sigh, Mr. Raskol turned to Francine—the smartest kid in our grade, hands down—for the next problem.

"Why don't you take number four, Ms. Stein?" he asked, in a tone that implicitly added *"and restore my faith in humanity."*

As Francine rattled off numbers, I kept my head low, but I knew the real danger was over. Mr. Raskol only humiliated students once per class period, which meant I could spend the next thirty-nine minutes pretending to follow along with relative ease.

When the three-thirty bell finally rang, Buddy and I headed for the exit, walking side by side.

"Want to come to my house?" he asked. "Mom just stocked up on Goldfish. We can play video games or shoot some hoops."

"Wish I could," I said. "But Mina signed me up for algebra tutoring."

Buddy's eyebrows bobbed upward.

"With some kid from Lakeview," I added.

"She got a *Fakeview* kid to teach you? Betcha ten dollars she shows up with Gucci glasses and her very own engraved protractor."

"Not an engraved protractor!" I cringed in mock horror. "Honestly, try not to miss me too much if I die of boredom."

"Why take the risk?" Buddy's brow furrowed. "You know," he said, "I could always tutor you."

I shrugged. "No offense, but Mina doesn't count A minuses as real A's."

Buddy ran his hand through his unruly brown hair, looking disappointed.

We headed out the school's double doors and into the bright, chilly day, where students milled around the parking lot, some waiting around for a ride home, others loitering and swapping gossip. I spotted my former teammate, Cami, talking to one of the new players who I'd never met. We made our usual *swish* signal at each other and grinned, but she didn't step away from her conversation.

Buddy snorted, diverting my attention. I followed his gaze to one of the school's windows. Jack Dover, a lunch mate of ours, stood inside a classroom with his entire face pressed against the smudged glass, his mouth stretched out in a goofy grimace. He had written HELP ME in erasable (I hoped) marker on the glass pane.

"Tell me he didn't get *another* detention today," I said.

"Two, actually. Probably three by now."

"Harsh." I groaned sympathetically. "Jack's in detention so much he deserves visitation rights."

We continued toward our neighborhood. The Lakeview tutor lived a mile past it, in the ritzier part of town. As we approached the Lucky Laundromat, Buddy slowed.

"Should we stop and say hi to your sister?" he asked.

I glanced inside. A few people were feeding quarters

into the machines or waiting on the benches while Mina bent over an ironing board, smoothing out the wrinkles on a button-down shirt. Her cell phone was trapped between her shoulder and the side of her head as she spoke to a customer.

"Not today." I hurried Buddy forward. After last night, I wasn't in the mood to be around Mina.

We passed the dingy corner store at the end of the street, with its displays of Choco Pies, *Nongshim Shin Ramyun* packs, and red-bean stuffed walnut cakes in the window. I wished I had remembered the money Jung-Hwa had given me so that I could buy a whole carton, but I had only two quarters on me.

Buddy waved goodbye as he turned onto his street, and I watched him go. I wanted to follow him back to his Gold-fish and graham-cracker-stocked pantry. Instead, I trudged forward until I left my neighborhood and arrived downtown.

I glanced into the big windows of Duo's Diner, envious of the kids inside sharing fries and milkshakes. On any other day, Buddy and I might be lounging at a booth, too; it was our favorite snack spot. Just pushing through the doors was like time traveling to an earlier era—one with vintage Coca-Cola signs on the wall, red leather booths, checkered flooring, and a working jukebox that played cheesy oldies. It seemed a small tragedy to waste a gorgeous day like today cooped up in some stuffy rich kid's house with math textbooks, and not here, sharing a triple chocolate sundae with Buddy.

At least I still had some time to enjoy the fresh air. Tutoring didn't start for another half hour, so I headed to the park and watched a pickup game for about twenty minutes. Too soon, I had to force myself to move on.

I double-checked the tutor's address, written on a slip of paper in Mina's scratchy handwriting. I had to assume the family was well-off, since they lived on the west side of the Alder Bridge, where the streets were lined with expensive houses—the big, posh ones with wide lawns and fancy gates.

As soon as I crossed the bridge, the grand homes loomed into sight. I walked all the way to the end of Satis Street to my destination—and that's when my jaw almost hit the ground. My new tutor lived in one of the largest houses in all of Victoria. I had biked past it once or twice but had never really stopped to marvel at the size. In fact, to call it a *house* seemed almost insulting. *Mansion* might have been a better word.

It was built of red brick in the Victorian style, with a wrap-around porch, gigantic shuttered windows, a round tower, and iron bars fencing off the front garden. Yet despite its grand exterior, whoever was in charge of the gardening must have been on permanent vacation. As I pushed open the heavy gates and headed up the stone path toward the front door, I noticed that weeds sprouted from every crack and crevice. The shrubs by the fence were wildly overgrown. Something thorny snagged my ankle and I had to tug my jeans free.

At the front door, I used a heavy bronze knocker shaped like a lion's head to announce my arrival. Minutes passed, but nobody answered. Frowning, I tried to peer in the window, but the curtains were drawn and I couldn't see anything.

I was about to knock again when the door flew open. I stepped back at the sight of a towering man in dark business pants with a crisp navy button-down shirt. He was about fifty, with salt-and-pepper hair, square black glasses, and cold blue eyes under heavy brows.

"No soliciting!" the man practically shouted.

I gulped. "Sorry. Do I have the wrong place? I'm supposed to be getting tutoring lessons with—" I checked Mina's note. "Someone named E. Haverford?"

The man's bushy eyebrows pressed together. "E?" Finally, he blinked. "Ah," he said. "You must mean Eliot. My apologies. I'm Eliot's father."

Mr. Haverford turned around and headed into the house, clearly expecting me to follow. After a moment of hesitation, I did, closing the solid oak door behind me. So, apparently my tutor wasn't going to be some nerdy girl with a personalized protractor . . . it was a nerdy boy with a personalized

24

protractor.

Hurrying forward to keep up with Mr. Haverford's long-legged pace, I couldn't help but gape at the huge entry hall, which was paneled in gloomy, dark wood. I tried not to stare as we passed through the enormous living room, which was . . . not at all what I expected.

The furniture was all fancy carved wood and silk and velvet, but it was also extremely *old*. Like it had been bought way back when the house was first built. The silk was faded and threadbare, and the velvet looked dusty. There was a giant painting over the mantelpiece, but it was covered with a piece of black cloth so that I couldn't see what it pictured. What appeared to be a grand piano squatted at the far end of the room, also covered in a dusty cloth. The stale air and the high ceilings made the place feel like a recently closed museum. Not the sort of place where you could picture kids living.

Mr. Haverford turned the corner into the dining room, and I darted after him . . . before skidding to an abrupt stop as I suddenly found myself gazing at the single most gorgeous boy I had ever seen.

4

THE GOLDEN BOY

"Hi," said the single most gorgeous boy I had ever seen. Seriously. His flawless skin seemed straight from a commercial for face wash, while his perfectly tousled blond hair could sell shampoo. "I'm Eliot."

Most of the time, I'm not aware of my heartbeat, but suddenly I could feel the rapid *thump-thump-thump* pulsing through my chest like the booming bass coming from a fancy stereo. It was so loud that Eliot could probably hear it, too. In fact, anybody living in the contiguous United States could have probably heard it.

This was Eliot Haverford, math genius?

I had been expecting a skinny, engineering-genius type with acne and a black Steve Jobs turtleneck. Not the star of a Disney channel movie. Why couldn't I stop staring? Well, actually, I knew why. And the answer was eyes so blue I temporarily lost my ability to blink.

Eliot was looking at me expectantly, and I realized that he had introduced himself and was now waiting for me to introduce myself back.

"I'm ... "

How were his eyes that blue?

"Pippa!" I finally managed to say, in a way that sounded far too enthusiastic. "My name is Pippa."

I stuck out my hand. Eliot stared at it for a moment, as though its presence baffled him. Finally, he extended his hand to shake mine. As he did, the crisp white cuff of his school uniform shirt pulled back to show a gleaming smart watch on his tanned wrist. My cheeks reddened with embarrassment as I suddenly noticed my ragged nails and chapped hands.

"Okay, Pippa." His tone made it obvious that his level of enthusiasm didn't match mine. That was fine. He would warm up to me once he got to know me better.

"Pippa, I'm sure you'll learn a lot from Eliot. He's at the top of his class in both math and science," Mr. Haverford told me. He gave Eliot's shoulder a light whack. "He's also on the basketball team this year. Hopefully he'll start working as hard on the court as he does in his studies."

Eliot smiled faintly.

"No way, what position are you?" I asked Eliot, eagerly leaning forward. "I play for Victoria Middle!" I decided not to mention I wasn't playing this season. "I'm a small forward."

Eliot shrugged. "I switch around," he said. "Anyway, we're here to do math, not talk sports."

I flushed again and glanced down at the thick maroon carpet so that he couldn't see the disappointed look in my eyes.

"Well, I'll leave you kids to it," Mr. Haverford said curtly.

He strode out of the room, leaving the two of us alone. I suppressed a sigh of relief; he didn't seem the friendliest. He was almost more intimidating than Mina.

I glanced around the room. It was dominated by heavy, dark wooden furniture and more paintings shrouded in black. A tall clock against the far wall ticked slowly and loudly. Otherwise the house was eerily silent.

"So, where do you want to start?" Eliot asked.

With your favorite hobbies, what you like to do on the weekends, whether or not you have a girlfriend . . .

"Well, we're doing linear equations. Unless you'd rather talk about basketball," I added with a hopeful grin.

He fixed me with a cool stare. "Why would I?"

Biting my lip, I opened my textbook. "Okay, linear equations."

Eliot flipped open his notebook to a fresh page, and began writing down sample problems. As he worked, he started lecturing about the best ways to find X, Y, and whatever other renegade letters might pop up. Mixing letters with numbers sounded genius when Eliot suggested it.

"Right," I said, nodding along.

I tried hard to concentrate, but I was too on edge. The house—well, the silence made me feel as if I should be whispering while the musty air made me want to sneeze. And Eliot! Besides being unreasonably cute, he was obviously really smart. He had an adorable way of furrowing his brow when he focused on a problem. He also had a habit, I noted, of fidgeting with one of the buttons on his shirt while explaining particularly difficult concepts.

He was still wearing his Lakeview uniform—a white shirt paired with a navy tie, khaki pants, and dark shoes—and although Buddy liked to make fun of mandatory school uniforms, Eliot had already converted me. I snuck a glance down at my own outfit. A plain red sweatshirt with frayed cuffs, ripped jeans, and my scuffed-up Converse. I hoped that Eliot thought the denim was "distressed" on purpose and wouldn't suspect the truth—that they were just old.

"Do you understand?" Eliot asked.

"What? Oh. Um . . . I think so?" I put down my pencil. "Actually, do you mind if we take a break? My hand is getting cramped."

He gave me that totally unnerving, blank look. "If you want."

Alrighty, then. I massaged my aching hand, and tried to keep the nervous sweating at bay. Part of me wished this tutoring session would end so I could scurry away in shame. But part of me didn't care how awkward I felt; as long as I could keep looking at Eliot, I never wanted to leave.

We sat in silence for a minute while I racked my brain for things to say. "So . . . the boys' basketball team at Lakeview is pretty good," I ventured at last.

Eliot tilted his head but didn't reply.

"You guys destroyed our team last season," I continued.

Eliot flipped a page in his notebook. "It's not surprising that Lakeview would crush Victoria Middle. I mean, come on."

He spat out the words *Victoria Middle* like it left a gross taste on his tongue. It made my cheeks heat up for the umpteenth time. By now, I'm sure he thought that's just how my face looked.

"But the girls' team at Lakeview loses to Victoria Middle every year," I shot back.

His expression darkened, making me wish I hadn't pointed that out.

Trying to recover, I hastily asked, "Have you gone to Lakeview your whole life?"

"Of course," he scoffed.

Why *of course*? "Is it all that different from public school?"

Eliot tilted his head and narrowed his eyes, like this was the most ridiculous question he had ever heard.

"Well, for one thing, Lakeview's scores on every state test are about twenty percent higher than any other school in western Massachusetts. We also have one of the best theater programs, and our debate club and our coding club have both been recognized at the national level," he drawled. "Not to mention, the boys' basketball team is one of the best in the entire state. *Of course* it's that different."

It was weird. I honestly didn't think Eliot meant to come off as rude—it was more like he didn't consider his words an insult. They were simple facts.

"Oh, and we don't have mystery meat in our cafeteria," he added, looking satisfied with this last proof of Lakeview's superiority. "I thought mystery meat was made up until I saw a documentary on it last month."

"Don't worry, no one eats that," I said, trying to play it cool. "I think they use it for spackle. It would explain the smell in the halls."

He let out a chuckle then looked surprised that he had laughed. His serious expression returned, and he immediately demanded, "Is your hand still cramping, or can we move on?" But his curt tone couldn't stop the warm glow spreading through my chest. I had managed to make him laugh! Sure, it had been a short one . . . but if I could do it once, I could do it again.

I picked up my pencil, and Eliot continued his lecture

on the importance of tracking down **X**, his voice clear and self-assured.

What would it be like to have his kind of confidence? Did you have to be rich? Did you have to go to Lakeview? I had a sudden vision of myself in the private school outfit—a khaki skirt, with a white button-down top, a navy sweater vest, and brown Oxfords. That's what Lakeview girls wore around town, and they always looked so polished. I stared down at my notebook, but in my mind I was sitting in Duo's across from Eliot, sharing some fries. He was laughing at the hilarious joke I'd just—

Bang! The sound of the front door slamming broke my daydream. I waited for someone to shout *hello*, but instead heard nothing but footsteps that faded away quickly.

"Was that your mom?" I ventured.

"No," Eliot said shortly.

O-kay . . . "You know, this house is so quiet," I said. "Should we put on some music? Sometimes it helps me con—"

"This tutoring is only going to help if you focus," Eliot cut me off.

"Right, sorry." Swallowing hard, I forced myself to concentrate on the math.

Fortunately, my embarrassment faded as the lesson

went on. I learned that as long as I didn't try to chat with him, everything would go smoothly. Eliot was really good at explaining things. To my surprise, I actually started to feel less confused.

At six exactly, Eliot closed the notebook and stood up. He started down the hallway toward the front door, looking over his shoulder at me expectantly.

"Oh," I said, scrambling to put my textbook back in my bag. I bounded to my feet. "I guess I'll see you next Tuesday?" I said as I scurried after him. I cringed at my tone of voice, which sounded annoyingly eager.

"I guess so," he said over his shoulder, already pulling open the front door. He held it open for me.

I stepped through and hesitated. "Well—" I began.

But he closed the door without letting me finish. I lingered on the doormat outside, staring at the wooden door.

What to make of Eliot Haverford? He was rude, for sure. Arrogant, definitely. He didn't seem to like me much at all. My shoulders slumped. So how come I really wanted him to?

I thought back to the moment he had laughed at my joke, how comically surprised he had looked. I wondered how often he laughed in a normal day.

Maybe I shouldn't take Eliot's brashness personally.

Maybe he just needed someone like me to show him how to have fun.

Perking up, I straightened my shoulders and started walking home. That was it. Eliot would teach me math, and I would teach him how to crack a smile.

5

ASPIRATIONS

Feint right, head left, three dribbles, and an easy layup. Buddy was so predictable. I tossed the ball to him, waited for him to move forward, then stole it mid-dribble.

Buddy kicked the asphalt, and I batted my eyelashes innocently.

The trick is to focus on your opponent's torso. Eyes can lie, and so can shoulders, feet, and heads. Buddy hadn't quite learned that yet. Not surprisingly, after a few more stolen shots, he slumped down in the middle of the court, his legs sprawled out, gasping for air.

"Giving up already?" I teased. "It's only 22-4."

"Everyone . . . loves . . . an underdog," Buddy panted, his entire body slick with sweat. I hadn't creamed him this badly in a while. "Watch out, Park. Next time . . . it's gonna be 22-6 at least."

Laughing, I helped him to his feet.

Ever since we'd been old enough to come to the park alone, Saturday mornings were reserved for games of one-on-one with Buddy. In the beginning, when Buddy had a lot more practice than me, I could barely nab a win. Now, I couldn't remember the last time I had lost. Either way, this was always the best two hours of the week for me.

I grabbed my water bottle, took a long swig, and passed it to Buddy. He gave me a grateful smile, and I noticed our eyes were about level. He was tall, but in the last few months, I had been sprouting up like a beanstalk. Now I was among the tallest girls in my grade. I liked it, but it made Mina resentful. Partly because it meant she had to buy me a new pair of shoes, but also because I was now taller than she was. As Omma liked to say (and as Mina hated to hear), "Pippa keeps growing up, and Mina keeps growing out."

Buddy handed my water bottle back and squinted over my shoulder. "That silver SUV has been sitting at the curb for like, ten minutes now, but no one's gotten out," he observed. "What's your guess? FBI?"

I turned and followed his gaze. The car was a luxury brand, with tinted windows so you couldn't see who was inside it. As I watched, it started up and drove away. The license plate said LKV1.

"Probably just lost." I shrugged. "Come on, let's go.

Mina wants me to work a couple hours at the laundromat today. I need fuel first."

The early cold snap of a few weeks ago had been replaced by warm weather, and I was feeling content as we set off for the other part of our Saturday tradition: ice cream sundaes at Duo's Diner.

We claimed a booth toward the back, and while Buddy ordered our usual, I dug up some quarters and headed to the jukebox.

The first time I looked at the jukebox at Duo's, I was surprised that there was no K-pop. Back then, I'd been obsessed with the bands that were huge in Korea—SHINee, Girl's Generation, Big Bang. But nobody besides Mina and Jung-Hwa ever listened to Korean music, and once I started middle school, it didn't take me long to realize that nobody even knew who G-Dragon was. I still sometimes blasted songs like "Hot Issue" and "I Am the Best"—but only when nobody was listening. In public, it was strictly tunes from the Top 50 charts.

Duo's jukebox, though, didn't have any songs, Korean or American, more recent than 1980, as far as I could tell. I went with one of Buddy's favorite rock classics, "Pinball Wizard" by The Who.

"Nice pick!" Mrs. Jecknell, the co-owner of Duo's,

danced over to us, two enormous ice cream sundaes in hand. Buddy and I always got one banana butterscotch and one hot fudge, ate them halfway, and then swapped.

I smiled at Mrs. Jecknell, glad that she was the one serving us today. She embodied the charm of the place with her smooth, rosy cheeks, boisterous laugh, and knack for remembering everybody's name. Everyone hoped to get her at their table instead of the other owner, her brother, Mr. Hine. If you got Mrs. Jecknell as a server, you got extra whipped cream and double cherries. Mr. Hine was more likely to serve up an impatient stare or a grumpy reminder not to spill on his counters.

"Cheers," Buddy said, *clinking* his spoon against mine. "I love this sunny weather," he added, giving a lazy stretch. "Let's get on the court every day this week."

"I'll try," I agreed. If I got up an hour early and did my Lucky Laundromat chores before school, Mina would probably let me play in the afternoons before homework. "Except for Tuesday, of course."

"Yeah. I still can't believe Mina is making you spend time with that Fakeview kid," he grumbled.

"I'm actually learning a lot. Not just about math," I said. "Eliot's been telling me all about Lakeview."

"Oh? And what did *Eliot* say?" Buddy asked, enunciating Eliot's name with a hard and definitive T.

I could tell from his tone that Buddy didn't *actually* want to hear about it, but I told him anyway. I'd had two tutoring sessions so far, and the more time I spent with Eliot, the more I got the feeling that he was right—Lakeview really was superior. Lakeview kids had opportunities I'd never even dreamed of. Even though Buddy still thought the students were snobs, I'd go there in an instant. If Jung-Hwa ever won the lottery, that is.

Also, not that I was keeping count or anything, but I'd made Eliot laugh twice last Tuesday. I loved the way his head tilted back when he chuckled.

"Well, besides the fact that Lakeview scores way better than Victoria Middle on every kind of testing, the coding and theater programs are practically Harvard level," I said. "And the sports! They have their own Olympic pool, squash and tennis courts, even a fencing coach. I have to admit, it sounds pretty great."

"The girls' basketball team isn't so good," Buddy replied curtly. "Remember how badly you guys beat them last year?"

I spooned a butterscotch-coated banana into my mouth, remembering that game. It was the one matchup that everyone knew mattered more than any other. Every year, on the first Friday of December, Victoria Middle went head-to-head against Lakeview. Last year's match had been my first time out on the court in my official Victoria Middle uniform and I'd been so proud. It wasn't exactly a landslide, but we'd won, 44-34. I'd scored nine points.

The very thought of that triumph made my throat tighten. How could Mina forbid me from playing on the team? It was the one thing I was really good at, and she had taken it away from me.

As Buddy and I switched sundaes, the front door of the diner opened and a cluster of boys trooped in. At the head of the pack was Eliot Haverford.

My breath hitched. Despite the frostiness of my sundae, my cheeks felt like they were on fire. Buddy spun around, following my stare. He might have even said something, but I wasn't up for conversation; I couldn't turn my attention away from Eliot's golden head.

As he scanned the booths, looking for somewhere to sit, our eyes met. I nodded in what I hoped was a cool, understated way.

Eliot paused for a moment, his face blank. Then he turned and walked to the opposite end of the diner, his posse close on his heels.

My stomach seized up. He hadn't waved at me. Hadn't smiled. Hadn't even blinked.

I licked my spoon clean of hot fudge and used it to peep at my reflection. *No wonder he didn't say hi,* I lectured myself. My dark hair was plastered to my forehead with sweat, and runny orange butterscotch outlined my lips. I was a disaster.

I put my spoon down. "Come on, let's get out of here," I muttered.

Buddy and I split the bill. With tax and a tip, we both ended up owing four dollars and fifty cents. I dumped three wrinkly ones and a handful of quarters onto the table—an entire week of laundry duties. Mina paid me a dollar for every ten pounds of washing, drying, and folding I completed, along with fifty cents for hand-washing garments. It wasn't much, but it covered ice cream every weekend, so I couldn't complain.

Eliot didn't look up as we left the diner.

Outside it was warm and bright. Buddy gave a pleased whistle.

"I still can't believe how nice it is outside," he said, stretching his arms above his head. "Bike ride tomorrow?"

"If my sister lets me."

My voice wasn't exactly cheerful, but Buddy didn't seem to notice as he turned for home. Heading back toward the Lucky Laundromat, I stopped into the Asian grocery store that stocked all my favorite Korean treats, fingering Jung-Hwa's five-dollar bill in my pocket.

I was stuffed from the sundae with Buddy, but in my

gloomy mood I wanted something to cheer me up, and a couple of red-bean walnut cakes were my best bet.

As I passed the magazine rack a cover caught my eye. The magazine was called *Tween Things*, and the cover showed a girl with perfect blond hair and green eyes staring moodily ahead. She was gorgeous. She was cool. Both things I wasn't.

If I looked like her, I bet Eliot would have said hello to me in the diner.

Neon type on the cover made promises like, "Learn Everything About Makeup" and "Cheap Chic." From a yellow bubble, a bold, cherry-colored headline read, "New School Year, New You: The Rules of Cool You Need to Know."

For a second, I thought about buying the magazine, but then I shook my head. Why waste my money? I wasn't blond, I wasn't cool, and I never would be. And now that I thought about it, I wasn't even in the mood for a walnut cake.

Stuffing the wrinkled five back into my pocket, I left the store and trudged toward the laundromat.

6

THE OPPORTUNITY

When I walked into the apartment later that afternoon, I was greeted by a spicy, vinegary, delicious smell and the sound of voices.

"So I told her, 'if you're not going to make your own kimchi, everyone knows to buy it from the pastor's wife." Our neighbor, Mrs. Lee, rapped on the kitchen table for emphasis as she spoke.

"*Samonim's* kimchi is the best. So sour," Jung-Hwa agreed. He glanced up from the stove as I entered the kitchen. "Pippa! Just in time. Does this need more *gochujang*?"

He held a spoonful of *kimchi-jjigae* toward me and I slurped the broth down, savoring the strong, spicy flavor. My stomach growled, reminding me that I'd eaten nothing but sugar for lunch.

"It's perfect." I was tempted to grab my own spoon

and keep eating, but I knew Jung-Hwa wouldn't let me dive in until dinnertime.

I filled a glass with tap water then sat down at the table. Before I had settled into my seat, a blur of brown and grey fur flew into my lap. It was Boz, Mrs. Lee's cat. Even though Mrs. Lee lived less than two minutes away, she never went anywhere without the scruffy Burmese. I scratched behind his ears, and he rewarded me with a contented purr.

"So, Pippa, your sister tells me you've been seeing a tutor for math. A boy name Eliot," Mrs. Lee said. Her black eyes snapped with interest. "One of the Haverfords." She pronounced the name like it had some special meaning.

"That's right," I confirmed, groaning inwardly. Mrs. Lee was . . . well, the polite way to say it was that she found other people's lives very interesting. *Nosy* would be another way to describe her. "Do you know them?"

"I've never met them, but of course I know *about* them," Mrs. Lee replied. "Such a tragedy!"

My heart thudded against my ribs. "What do you mean?" Had something happened to Eliot?

"It was years ago," Mrs. Lee said. "Back when I was just a girl."

I didn't know how old Mrs. Lee was, but I did know she'd come here from Korea as a teenager in the 1960s. Whatever she was talking about must have occurred long before

Eliot was even born. Relaxing, I leaned in closer. "What happened?" I asked, suddenly feeling a little bit nosy, too.

"It was a catastrophe," Mrs. Lee said. She spoke in a somber tone, but I could tell by the excited glint in her eyes that she enjoyed her role as storyteller. "It was in all the newspapers, on the TV—my English was not too good then, but I read all the stories anyway. They were a very important family in this town, you know. We were all shaken by the accident."

"Accident?" I echoed.

Jung-Hwa clicked his tongue sympathetically and poured more tea into Mrs. Lee's cup.

"The Haverford daughter, I think her name was Evelyn, was playing with the Boston Symphony." Mrs. Lee's eyes crinkled up as she thought back. "Her first big performance. Her brother—Eliot's grandfather—and his wife were on their way to see it, and some maniac ran their car off the road. Left their little baby son an orphan."

Their baby son: That would mean Mr. Haverford, Eliot's father.

"That's terrible!" Jung-Hwa exclaimed. "I hope they caught the driver."

"It gets worse." Mrs. Lee paused to take a long sip of tea. Anxious for her to go on, I couldn't stop my leg from bobbing. "Evelyn's father, old man Haverford, had a stroke when he heard the news," Mrs. Lee finally continued. "They say he blamed the daughter. Didn't approve of her musical career, you see. The poor thing lost her whole family, all in one go!"

"What about old man Haverford's wife?" Jung-Hwa asked.

Mrs. Lee waved a hand. "Oh, she died years before any of this."

I wanted to get back to the tragic daughter. "What happened to Evelyn?" I asked. "She must have been devastated."

"I'm not sure," Mrs. Lee admitted. "The Haverford house over on Satis Street was empty for a long time. Boarded up. Then I guess someone must have moved back in, because the boards came off. But I don't know what happened to Evelyn." She sipped her tea. "Is that where you get tutored, Pippa?"

I nodded and sat back in my chair. Wow! So Eliot had a tragic family history. I wondered where Evelyn Haverford was now. She must be an old lady—even older than Mrs. Lee. Was she still alive? Did she live in Victoria?

The front door slammed, and Boz sprung from my lap, leaving claw marks on my knees. A minute later Mina bustled into the kitchen. She greeted Mrs. Lee, and I took the chance to escape to my room.

I showered then lay down on my unmade bed and stared up at the cracking paint of my ceiling. I couldn't stop thinking about Eliot and his family.

"Pippa!" Mina called from the kitchen. "Come set the table! It's time to eat."

Trying to push Eliot from my mind, I headed back to the kitchen. I didn't talk much during dinner. I was still thinking about Eliot and his Great-Aunt Evelyn. Could I ask him about her? It might get him to open up to me. But then again, it might just make him mad.

You won't know how he'll react unless you do it, I finally decided. I imagined the heartfelt conversation I'd have with him. Eliot would start out grumpy but when he saw how much I cared, his walls would come crashing down and soon enough we would be holding hands as he poured his heart out to me.

Yes, it would definitely be worth the risk.

Monday morning, I slept through my alarm, so I didn't get a chance to work at the laundry until after school. When I got home, sweaty from the heat of all the dryers, I could hear Mina and Jung-Hwa talking in the living room. They fell silent as I walked in. Both of them stared at me.

My heart sank. "What? What did I do now?"

Silently, Mina handed me a thick envelope slit open at the top. Inside was a piece of cream-colored paper with fancy letterhead in red ink. The emblem at the top looked familiar — then I realized it was the same one on Eliot's uniform.

"This is from Lakeview?" Why were they sending letters to my family?

"It's a scholarship offer!" Jung-Hwa exclaimed. His chest puffed out with pride, and his wide grin nearly split his face. "They want you to come for a tour!"

Jung-Hwa eagerly went on, but his voice faded into the background as my eyes flew over the words.

Dear Mr. and Mrs. Kim,

On behalf of The Lakeview School, we are pleased to extend a scholarship opportunity to your ward, Pippa Park. As you know, since 1923, Lakeview has been raising some of the finest future leaders, innovators, and thinkers of the new generations.

In an effort to enrich our girls' sports teams, we have been reaching out to talented players in the community with strong recruitment potential. Pippa's basketball skills have been recommended to us most highly, and we are prepared to offer her a full scholarship to our program on the stipulation that Pippa is able to maintain a minimum GPA of 3.0 while playing as a member of the Lakeview Jaguars.

Please let us know when you'd like to come in and discuss this unique offer and take a tour of Lakeview.

We look forward to your reply.

With best wishes,
Alyson Moore
Chair of Recruitment

I read the letter twice.

Was this a joke? The only time I'd had any interaction with Lakeview had been at the season opener last year, which had taken place at Victoria Middle. I'd never been to the Lakeview campus. Did someone on the team remember me from that game?

"We're so proud of you, our little *gangaji*," Jung-Hwa said, tweaking my cheek. Gangaji meant puppy in Korean. Jung-Hwa always said that I reminded him of one because of my boundless energy. "And your Omma will be, too."

I looked from Jung-Hwa to Mina, bewildered. "How did this happen?"

"We were hoping you could tell us," Mina said, speaking for the first time. She looked mystified and a little suspicious. "We certainly didn't have anything to do with it."

"Well, I didn't either!" I said. "The only person from Lakeview I even know is—"

I stopped short. Eliot? Could Eliot have had something to do with this?

Surely not. I'd tried to talk to him about basketball more than once, but he wasn't interested. And he'd never seen me play, so he couldn't have any idea whether I was good or not.

"—Is your math tutor," Mina finished for me. She narrowed her eyes in thought. "Maybe the tutoring program is a way to identify strong potential students. It seems strange, but . . . "

"Then you're responsible for this, after all, yeobo," Jung-Hwa said, beaming at her. "Since you set up the tutoring."

My hand holding the letter started to shake, and a weird buzzing filled my ears. Could it be? Eliot Haverford was the only link I could think of between me and Lakeview. Was it possible he'd recommended me for the scholarship?

I didn't quite dare believe it—but a bubble of hope started to swell inside me.

I would have a chance to go to Lakeview, with its incredible facilities and its great test scores. Maybe I'd even join the coding team! I thought giddily. Clearly, stranger things did happen.

And above everything else, maybe Eliot really did like me after all . . . .

With a squeal, I launched myself at Mina, wrapping her in an excited hug. I kissed her on the cheek, and then wrapped my arms around Jung-Hwa's big, solid body before hurrying to my room. I needed to tell Buddy the good news.

Clutching the letter in one sweaty hand, I texted Buddy with the other.

Buddy! U won't BELIEVE what just happened
Mr. Raskol gave you an A?

I'm going to private school!!

What?

Lakeview wants me on the basketball team! They're giving me a scholarship!

There was a long pause.

But Mina will never let you play, Buddy wrote at last.

She has to! It's part of the scholarship offer!

Another long pause.

Wow. That's random.

Random? Was that all he had to say? I felt a little hurt. Then another text popped up.

But cool, of course. How did they find out about you, exactly?

Should I tell Buddy that I thought it might be through Eliot? I decided against it. I wasn't sure of that and anyway, Buddy already seemed less than enthusiastic about my news.

Have no idea, I wrote.

I waited a couple of minutes, but he didn't text back.

I tugged at my ponytail with a frown. Buddy's response cast a slight cloud over my happiness, but I tried not to take it personally. After all, if he told me he was off to a fancy private school without me, I'd definitely feel hurt, too. I would just have to hope he would get over it sooner rather than later.

But meanwhile, there was something else I needed to

do. I checked my pocket to make sure I still had Jung-Hwa's five-dollar bill. Then I hurried out of the apartment. "Back in two minutes!" I yelled over my shoulder.

I ran down to the Asian grocery on the corner and made a beeline for the magazine rack. *Tween Things* was still there, with the gorgeous blond girl still pouting on its cover. And that tantalizing article: "New School Year, New You!"

I grabbed the magazine, slapped my money down on the counter, and waited impatiently for my change. As soon as it was in my hand, I raced home again.

Mina stared at me as I dashed through the living room. "Homework," I panted, and zipped into my room. It was the truth, though my sister might not see it that way.

Grabbing a highlighter, I threw myself on my bed and prepared to get down to business. I definitely needed to learn those Rules of Cool now that I would be going to Lakeview.

It was time to become the interesting, confident, private school version of Pippa. The one who wore a crisp school uniform and styled her hair like the girl on the magazine. The one who Eliot would fall for.

Propping my chin in my hands, I started reading. I had a lot of learning to do.

7

FIRST GLIMPSE

My Lakeview tour was scheduled for 1:30 p.m. that Tuesday. At exactly 12:45, Mina met me at Victoria Middle, and we headed to the nearest bus stop. She paid for our fares, and we slid into two seats as the bus jolted forward. Trying not to psych myself out, I stared blankly at the long stretch of road. My stomach fluttered. Normally, I would be elated to ditch class, but today I was too nervous to enjoy it.

"Pippa," Mina snarled after a few moments.

"What?"

She placed her hand on my knee, and I realized I had been bobbing my leg up and down.

"Relax," she commanded. "It's just a tour. Not even you could mess this up."

What a great pep talk from the world's best confidence coach. I tried to swallow, but my mouth was too dry.

I forced myself to sit still and started mentally reviewing the Rules of Cool from *Tween Things*. The first one, "Fake It Till You Make It," was about acting confident even when you were unsure of your own coolness. It made sense on paper but seemed less practical in reality. What if I acted like a really confident dork? Would people think I was fun and quirky or would they just laugh at me?

Rule 2 seemed easier. "Leave 'em Wanting More" basically said that you shouldn't appear too eager to make new friends. It might seem desperate. Rule 2 kind of went with Rule 4, "Maintain Some Mystery." *So don't immediately tell everyone your entire life story, Pippa,* I counseled myself. *Let them wonder about you.*

Now . . . what was Rule 3? The bus slid to a bumpy stop before I could come up with it. Mina stood. "We're here."

Gulping, I followed her off the bus.

We were in the fancy part of town, out past Eliot's house. The block we were on didn't seem to have any houses—just a long stone wall, about as tall as my shoulder, that ran along the sidewalk. In the middle of the block, brass gates stood open. The entrance to the school. We walked through and started up a flagstone path shaded by rows of stately trees on either side.

Lakeview didn't look like any other school I'd ever seen. It was a huge, rambling mansion built of mellow old brick. Tall windows set off by dark green shutters looked out on a sweeping lawn. To the right, a parking lot full of school buses and cars was half-hidden by a line of hedges. To the left were a couple of other brick buildings, one that said *Petersen Sports Center* in gold letters on the glass door. Wow. A separate building just for sports?

I stopped walking to take it all in.

Why did I think for a moment that I could belong here? I shook my head. *This is where the rich kids go to school. Not someone like me.*

"Fake it till you make it." Who was I kidding? I'd never fit in here.

"Pippa, get moving. We don't want to be late." Mina plowed ahead.

My gaze swept the campus one last time, and I forced my insecure thoughts to the back of my mind. This place was too amazing. I *had* to go to school here. *No one needs to know I'm poor,* I thought, catching up to my sister. *And once they get to know me, they'll like me so much, it won't matter.*

We reached the building's entrance.

This is it.

Inhaling, I tugged down the hem of my dress. It was a simple navy-blue sheath that I had worn exactly twice: once at Christmas Mass, and again at a wedding for one of Mina's friends. It might not have been the most glamorous pick but,

55

as Mina said, at least it made me look "presentable." No way I could wear my ripped-up jeans and faded T-shirts to Lakeview.

"Don't forget to be polite, but do ask questions," Mina reminded me.

I bobbed my head, and we stepped through the glass double-doors into an airy, light-filled space. Glass-fronted cases lined the walls between the windows and held a mix of photos, trophies, and school memorabilia. On one side was a seating area with worn but comfortable-looking chairs and a long wooden bench. On the other was a reception desk with a smiling red-haired woman behind it. "You look like you're here for a tour," she called as we gazed around uncertainly.

We approached the desk. "We have an appointment with the principal," Mina said, sounding a little stiff. "At one-thirty. Mina Kim and Pippa Park."

"Ah, yes. If you'll give me a moment, I'll let the head-master know you're here." The woman stood and disappeared through one of the doors behind her desk.

Headmaster. Not principal. I watched as Mina's cheeks reddened slightly. It occurred to me that she might be feeling intimidated. I couldn't remember a time when my tough, no-nonsense sister had ever felt nervous.

Mina checked the time on her phone while I wandered over to one of the glass trophy cases. A framed photo of a boys' soccer team hung next to a brass cup, and my heart skipped a beat as I spotted Eliot in the back row, center. Everyone in the photo was smiling except him—he looked straight into the camera with slightly narrowed eyes, as if he was challenging the photographer.

"Pippa?"

I turned to see a broad-shouldered woman emerge from the same door the receptionist had gone through. She wore navy trousers with a white blouse and a chic striped blazer. Her short brown hair was just starting to show gray at the temples.

"I'm Joanna Thorpe, the assistant headmistress," she said, holding out a hand.

I quickly wiped my sweaty palms on my dress before shaking her hand.

"*Assistant* headmistress?" Mina repeated, sounding accusing.

"You must be Pippa's sister." Ms. Thorpe turned to-ward Mina. "I apologize, but the Head had an unexpected schedule conflict. I'm here to meet with you in his absence."

Ms. Thorpe steered us into a tastefully decorated office and motioned for us to take a seat. As I did, I looked through the window. Outside, beyond the sports center, a small lake sparkled in the sun. Of course—that must be the lake in *Lakeview*. Duh!

"Thank you for coming in today, ladies," said Ms.

Thorpe, and I refocused my attention. "We wanted to review the requirements with both of you, just to ensure that Pippa is a good match for Lakeview, as well as the other way around."

I wanted to yell, "I'm a good match! I'm a perfect match!" Instead, I plucked a lemon drop from the jar on her desk and rolled it around in my hand, trying to ignore Mina's dirty look.

"First of all, after studying your academic records, I see that your math scores leave something to be desired," Ms. Thorpe said, her gentle voice sounding genuinely concerned.

Mina clucked righteously, and I winced.

"That's true," I agreed, thinking fast. "Fortunately, I'm enrolled in the Lakeview tutoring program for math, as you probably know."

My chest puffed out an inch. That sounded almost decent.

"Oh, you are?"

I looked at Ms. Thorpe in surprise. Since tutoring with Eliot had helped me get this scholarship—or so I suspected—it seemed strange she didn't know about it already. But before I could explain further, she continued.

"Good. Very good. Of course, part of why we set up this offer is because of your basketball skills," she said. "But we also believe strongly in our duty to the Victoria community. The tutoring program is part of that commitment, and so is this offer. You're not just here to play sports. You're here to learn."

"You hear that?" Mina looked completely sold.

"That's why our scholarship offer is contingent on you playing basketball *and* maintaining a 3.0 GPA for the semester," Ms. Thorpe added. She looked at me to make sure I was paying attention. "That includes your math grade."

I felt sweat pop out along my hairline. Yes, the bit about the GPA had been in Lakeview's offer letter, but sitting here with Ms. Thorpe in her pristine office all of a sudden made it seem more serious. They really meant it.

"I can do that," I said with as much confidence as I could muster. "It won't be a problem."

The corners of Ms. Thorpe's mouth turned up. "I know you can."

"I'll make sure she does," Mina murmured.

"Now. Basketball practice is immediately after school Monday through Friday," Ms. Thorpe explained. "Coach Ahmad will watch you play on your first day before she decides how you'll fit into the team."

Ms. Thorpe handed over my schedule and locker combo just as dramatic classical music chords flowed through the speakers.

"There's the sixth period bell," she said, smiling. "Can you name that tune?"

I shook my head, intimidated. At least it sounded nicer than the tooth-shatteringly loud bell at Victoria Middle.

"It's Beethoven's Symphony No. 5," Ms. Thorpe said,

looking slightly disappointed. "Not to worry, you'll learn more about the world's most important musical figures now that you're here at Lakeview."

"Great," I said, wondering if anyone at this school knew a thing about K-Pop.

"Now, while I go over some details with your sister, you can take the official tour." Ms. Thorpe stood up. "One of our students, Olive Giordano, is going to show you around. She's been here since kindergarten, so she knows all the ropes."

Since kindergarten? I wondered then remembered that Lakeview went from K to eight. "Okay," I said to Ms. Thorpe, but my hands started to sweat. I hadn't prepared myself for a first encounter with one of my new classmates. What if she hated me immediately?

At least Mina wasn't coming on the tour with me, I told myself. This was my new start, and I didn't want the other kids' first impression of me to be my older sister screaming at me in the hallways.

Ms. Thorpe held open the door, clearly signaling it was time for me to leave. With a murmured *thank you*, I headed back into the lobby. I hadn't managed to take two steps forward when a sallow-skinned, dark-haired girl rushed over.

"Olive Giordano, student ambassador," she introduced herself, her voice nasal.

"Hi, I'm Pippa. I'm—" I said, trying to introduce myself, but she was already talking again.

"When I heard there was going be a new kid, I just had to be the one to show you around—and not just because it got me out of class. Ha! We don't get many newbies here. It's exciting . . . you'll have a lot of eyes on you." Olive looked pleased at the thought.

"Come on," she said. She seized my arm, the tiny baubles on her silver charm bracelet tinkling lightly as she pulled me forward.

As we navigated the hallways, Olive pointed out landmarks, like the cafeteria—which was originally a ballroom, she told me—and the auditorium, while babbling about everything from the worst and best teachers to the tastiest lunch options. When she started ranking the cutest boys, her words faded as my thoughts drifted to Eliot.

He was somewhere in this school at this very moment. Even though everyone was in class, I kept hoping to see him turn the corner or pop out of one of the bathrooms.

"Let's head over to the sports center," Olive said, snapping me back to reality. "I heard you're a basketball recruit." Her tone lowered to a whisper, as if this were supposed to be confidential information.

"Yeah," I said, not wanting to talk myself up, but unable to hide my enthusiasm. "I've been playing since—"

"Our boys' team is really good," Olive interrupted then reeled off some stats about their rankings.

As we entered the sports center I inhaled the warm,

moist air. It smelled like chlorine. "The pool's downstairs," Olive informed me. "It's olympic-sized."

I nodded, figuring if I didn't say anything, she couldn't interrupt me again. To the left of the doors was a glassed-in room with mats and weights and what looked like a climbing wall at one end. Straight ahead was the gymnasium itself. Olive led me in and I stared in happy amazement.

High windows all around let in tons of autumn sunlight, which gleamed warmly off the polished wood floor. Besides basketball hoops at either end, there were practice hoops and backboards along the sidelines. Dark-red bleachers lined each wall. The whole place was absolutely beautiful. Even wearing a dress, with no basketball in sight, I got a rush just from being on the court. I closed my eyes. I could practically hear the cheers of the fans. If I was lucky, they'd be cheering for me.

". . . last year, but I practiced all summer, and this year I finally made the team!"

Absorbed in my own thoughts, I'd only caught the end of what Olive had said. I turned to her in surprise. "You're on the basketball team?"

"Yep," Olive said. "I can't wait to be teammates! I can just tell you and I are going to be friends."

I smiled weakly. I guess it was nice that Olive seemed to like me so much, but would she actually like me once she got to know me? I had a feeling her friendliness had more to do with me being a new kid than my actual personality. Especially since she hadn't asked me a single thing about myself since we met.

The next stop on the tour was the journalism club.

"I used to be in here all the time when I published the school newspaper," Olive said. "But once I made the basketball team, I didn't have time for it anymore. Hey! I just got an idea—I could write an article about you so kids could get to know you!"

"I don't think—" I started, but was interrupted by a different classical song that came on over the speakers.

Olive grimaced. "The bell already? Great, now the halls will be packed." She looped her arm through mine. "So we don't get separated in the crowd," she told me.

As we walked through the main building I wondered what Olive meant by "the crowd." Maybe fifty kids emerged from the four classrooms on either side of the hall. That meant that each class had about twelve or thirteen students in it. I shook my head. At Victoria Middle, each class had at least thirty.

As we entered the front hall again I caught a glimpse of an extra-tall figure with a shock of salt-and-pepper hair whisking around a corner. My eyes widened. Wasn't that Eliot's father, Mr. Haverford? Was Eliot getting picked up early today?

Olive pulled me along. Although Mr. Haverford

disappeared from sight, my mind lingered on Eliot. I hoped he wasn't sick. It was Tuesday, which meant that I'd see him later for tutoring. I was bursting to tell him my news about going to Lakeview and see how he reacted.

My pulse quickened as I thought: *I am a Lakeview student!*

It hadn't fully sunk in until this very moment, but now I wanted to throw my head back and shout my happiness to the world.

I'm going to do everything right, I vowed. *I'll rule the basketball court. I'll sit with the cool kids at lunch. I'll learn about the great composers. I'll even ace every math test. Eliot will have no choice but to like me.*

I beamed. *Today, the new Pippa Park is born!*

8

IMPRESSIONS

The trip to Eliot's house for tutoring later that day felt momentous. In one short week I'd be starting at *his school*.

I had already begun working on my resolution to do everything right. I'd found an online recording of that Beethoven symphony they played to announce periods at Lakeview, and I was listening to it on my headphones as I walked through the weedy front yard of Eliot's house. It wasn't exactly SHINee, but it wasn't terrible, either.

As I walked up onto the porch, I noticed a silver SUV sitting in the driveway. The license plate read LKV1. I frowned, trying to think where I'd seen it before.

Then it hit me. That was the car that had been parked by the basketball court last weekend!

My thoughts raced. Everything was coming together now. Eliot *had* seen me play—he must have been in the car with his dad that day. That was why he'd recommended me for the scholarship. It really had been him!

As I rang the doorbell my heart sang. He did like me. He had to!

I pushed my headphones down around my neck as Eliot opened the door.

"Hey." He ran a hand through his hair. "Um, listen—"

But I couldn't contain myself. "Thank you, thank you!" I cried. On impulse, I moved forward to hug him. "I'm so excited!"

"What are you doing?" He jerked backward, looking shocked, and one of his buttons snagged my headphone cord. The jack came unplugged from my phone and loud orchestral music blasted out from the phone speaker. An expression of utter horror came over Eliot's face.

"What is that racket?" a sharp voice demanded from the dim interior of the house.

"Turn that thing off! Turn it off now!" Eliot said in a low, furious voice.

Stunned, I fumbled at my phone. I swiped to open it, but the screen froze. As I jabbed at it, Beethoven's thunderous chords kept blaring out.

"Eliot!" the sharp voice screeched. Just as I finally managed to silence the music, a tall, bony old woman stalked into the foyer. I froze in the act of tucking my phone into my backpack. I knew it was rude to stare, but I just couldn't help it.

Her white hair was pinned into a dramatic, poufy hairdo that perched on the top of her head like a mushroom. She wore a long black gown that glittered as she moved, and a filmy black shawl hung from her shoulders. She had on black, elbow-length gloves. A rope of pearls glistened at her throat. Why was she so dressed up in the middle of the afternoon?

She eyed me as though I were a bit of garbage that had blown in through her door. "Who is this?"

Eliot's face smoothed into a blank mask. "This is Pippa Park," he said to the old lady. "I'm tutoring her in math. Pippa, this is my great-aunt Evelyn."

"Uh—hello," I said, awed. Great-Aunt Evelyn! The violinist Mrs. Lee had told me about, the one whose family had all died. *Should I offer to shake hands? Should I curtsy?* Somehow that seemed more appropriate, given the way she was dressed. But I didn't know how to curtsy.

While these thoughts were going through my head, the old lady was looking me up and down coldly. Now she said, "You may call me Miss Haverford."

"Okay," I agreed meekly.

"I'm afraid Eliot hasn't got time to tutor you today," Miss Haverford announced. "He has some duties here at home."

"Uh—" I glanced at Eliot for confirmation, but he just stared blandly back at me.

"Was there something else?" Miss Haverford's tone was icy.

My shoulders slumped and I shook my head. I didn't think I would win an argument with this lady. "No, uh, I guess I'll be going then."

"Eliot will see you next week," Miss Haverford said as I turned to go.

Next week! The thing I'd wanted to talk to Eliot about—me going to Lakeview—had completely flown out of my head. But now I remembered.

I spun back around. "I just wanted to say—I'm really happy. About going to Lakeview. And the scholarship and all. So thank you. And see you Monday, at school."

Eliot's head tilted and his eyes narrowed. His mouth opened. But before he could say anything, his great-aunt slammed the door in my face.

. . .

On Monday morning, a huge breakfast spread awaited me on the kitchen table: oatmeal topped with brown sugar, cinnamon, and bananas; salted almonds to eat alongside; a plate of freshly sliced mango; a full glass of orange juice, and a cylindrical slab of yeot. Jung-Hwa had even taken the time to put out napkins and silverware—all before he left for his six a.m. shift at the factory.

It was so sweet of him that I wished I had more of an appetite, but I couldn't stomach more than a few pieces of fruit, as well as a bite of yeot. I broke off a small piece, forcing myself to chew the sweet, taffy-like confection. Yeot was supposed to give you good luck, especially with academics. I wasn't hugely superstitious, but I didn't want to risk anything today.

That thought in mind, I touched the Lakeview emblem on the left side of my blazer, my fingers tracing the outline of the shield. Even the embroidery seemed sophisticated and serious. Just like the new me. I studied my reflection in the toaster. With my immaculate white blouse and khaki skirt, I already looked like Pippa Park version 2.0. That was half the battle, right? *Fake it till you make it?*

"Let's go," Mina said, grabbing the keys. "You can't be late for your first day."

I grabbed my backpack and hurried after her to the car. In the days ahead, I'd either make the long walk to school alone or take the school bus, but on this special occasion Jung-Hwa had offered to use public transportation and leave Mina the old, battered Subaru.

As she started the engine, I thought about the fourth

69

Rule of Cool from my magazine: "Maintain Some Mystery." It made sense, even though it seemed shady. Pippa Park, average student from Victoria Middle, who lived in a shabby apartment and worked in a laundromat, was not popular-girl material. But at Lakeview I could be anyone, as long as they didn't find out the total truth about me. Eliot was the only one who knew I was on a scholarship, and I didn't think he'd tell anyone. He wasn't much of a talker.

"Are you nervous?" Mina asked, interrupting my thoughts.

I looked up, and a sudden cramp twisted my stomach. We were already halfway to Lakeview.

"No," I lied.

Mina glanced at my hands, balled up into fists so tight that my knuckles were turning white.

"Let me guess. You're worried about making new friends, or if the other kids will like you, right?" she said, surprising me with her accuracy. "Well, don't be. Focus on your grades. Remember, if you lose your scholarship because of low test scores, you'll be back at Victoria Middle."

I gnawed the inside of my cheek. As if my heart rate wasn't high enough.

"Now remember," Mina said as we rolled into the parking lot. "Pay attention in class. You're not here to socialize, you're—"

"Here to study," I finished.

"And stay—"

"Out of trouble, because detention marks might also make me lose the scholarship."

"And Pippa? Last thing: I'm proud of you."

I raised my eyebrows. Now that was a part of her lecture I didn't have memorized.

"Take this and hurry up," Mina said.

She passed me my green lunchbox. On a yellow sticky note, Jung-Hwa had written, "Good luck on your first day!" with a smiley face. Climbing out of the car, I thanked Mina for the ride, straightened my blazer, and hurried inside.

The front lobby was crowded with students in blazers, backpacks slung over their shoulders, talking and laughing. A few eyed me curiously as I walked, trying to remember the way to my locker. It was downstairs on the basement level, but how did I get down there?

I turned down the hallway to the right, realizing my mistake only after I'd passed the journalism room. Starting to sweat, I hurried in the opposite direction. A pair of girls carrying a giant papier-mâché praying mantis gave me dirty looks as I nearly ran into them.

There! I pushed through a door marked "stairwell," ran down the steps, and skidded to a stop in front of my locker, feeling victorious. I leaned down to pull up my knee socks, which had begun to droop, and then straightened back up. Now, what was the combination again? 9-04-16? 17-9-05?

Just as I finally entered the correct code, a burst of classical music came through the speakers. I glanced around to see the hall had emptied completely.

I stashed my backpack inside my locker and rushed to find my math classroom. I slipped through the door, hoping to claim a seat without being noticed by the teacher.

Not a chance.

"Late to the semester, and late to my class," said the teacher, a tiny woman with platinum-blond hair. "I certainly hope this isn't a pattern."

Oh, no! Another Mr. Raskol? "No, definitely not." I blushed. "Sorry."

She winked at me and my back muscles relaxed.

"I'm Mrs. Rogers," she said. "Welcome. Before you find a seat, will you please introduce yourself to the class?"

Suddenly, more than a dozen pairs of eyes were staring at me. Sweat made my hands cold and clammy.

"Hi. My name is Pippa," I said, forcing myself to smile. I stared out at the faces, wondering what they were thinking. Could they sense that behind my toothy smile I was freaking out?

Confident, upbeat, and laid-back, I coached myself. "Pippa Park," I said, more assertively this time. "Nice to meet everyone."

With a small wave that I hoped said "I belong here," I scanned the room for a free seat, and slid into one near the back, toward the windows. Nobody snickered at me, making me feel irrationally pleased that I hadn't messed up.

Mrs. Rogers scrawled a loopy "Welcome, Pippa" on the chalkboard then began to lecture about linear equations. Most of the students kept their eyes on her—but a girl a few rows over kept glancing at me. She had smooth, dark brown skin and long braided hair with a gold-colored fabric hair tie wrapped around her left wrist. On the right side of her blazer, she wore a delicate sailboat brooch adorned with tiny, shimmery red gems. She was the prettiest girl in the room, and she seemed to be sizing me up, which made me nervous.

Confidence, Park. Fake it. I forced myself to hold her gaze and smile.

Three seconds ticked by.

Four.

Excruciating.

Five.

The girl smiled back.

Before I could react, she turned her eyes forward, and that was that. What was behind that smile? I cocked my head uncertainly. Had that been a successful encounter—or a terrible one? And why was it so hard to tell the difference between the two?

Exhaling, I tried to pay attention to Mrs. Rogers, who was now explaining the slope-intercept form. But it was hard. My fingers tracing the Lakeview emblem on my blazer, I looked back over at the girl with the sailboat brooch. She *oozed* cool. Could someone like me *really* be friends with her?

Remember the Rules of Cool, I told myself. Rule 3: "Cool Takes Courage." It said not to be afraid to put yourself out there. You couldn't tell whether someone would be your friend if you didn't even try to talk to them.

As I sat there I made a decision: After class, I would introduce myself to Sailboat Girl. I wouldn't push—I'd just walk up, say, "Hi, I'm Pippa," and see what happened. Cool, casual, no big deal. Right?

So why did I feel like I was going to faint?

9

THE MAKE OR BREAK

As it turned out, my nervousness was for nothing. I didn't have the chance to talk to Sailboat Girl at all. After class, Mrs. Rogers called me up to her desk to talk to me about my math background. "Remember, if you're struggling with the class, communication is key," she told me. "I can't help you if I don't know you need help."

"Okay," I said, my cheeks reddening. She must have checked out my records from Victoria Middle. What else did she know about me? Did she know about my scholarship deal? Probably. Did she know I was poor? I hoped not.

Mrs. Rogers looked at me for another minute then smiled. "All right, Pippa, you'd better get going," she said. "Good luck with the rest of your classes."

Does she mean I'm going to *need* luck? I wondered. My stomach churned.

My next class turned out to be Earth Science. Not very interesting, but not very hard either. After that, I had English and then it was time for lunch.

I drew a deep breath before I walked into the big, high-ceilinged cafeteria. Who would I sit with?

As it turned out, Olive waylaid me on the first step I took into the room.

"Pippa! Come sit with us!" she said.

"Okay," I said gratefully.

I followed her to her table, also occupied by a girl with braces and another with long, curly red hair. After Olive introduced me to Veronica and Kelly, I started unpacking my lunchbox. Jung-Hwa had given me a Tupperware full of leftovers, a juice box, and a Choco Pie for dessert. I ate the Choco Pie first, and then opened up the plastic container.

"What is *that*?" Olive asked. She stared at the container with one raised eyebrow.

"Fried chicken, kimchi, and rice," I said.

"What's kimchi?" Kelly asked.

"Spicy fermented cabbage," I said.

"Fermented?" Olive wrinkled her nose. "I was wondering what the smell was."

I flushed. Hastily, I put the lid back on the container and stuffed it back into my lunchbox. My stomach growled in protest.

"Here, have some of my fries," Olive said, sliding some over. Munching, she went on, "You're lucky I grabbed you fast, you know. You could have ended up sitting with the chess geeks or something."

I followed Olive's finger to a group of kids sitting a few tables over. To me, they didn't look any more or less remarkable than Olive and her friends.

Olive leaned in. "Pro tip. Who you eat lunch with is very important. If you eat with the wrong people, you're toast." She winked at me. "Don't worry, you're safe with us."

"Oh," I said, adding this to my list of worries. *Don't let anyone know about the scholarship. Don't let them find out you're poor. And now ... don't sit at the wrong lunch table.* "Thanks."

Olive spent the rest of the lunch period gabbing about the highlights of her day, from the new charm her mom had gotten her, to the amazing essay she had turned in, barely requiring more than a nod from me, Kelly, or Veronica the entire time.

The only other thing that happened was that I spotted Sailboat Girl on the other side of the room. She sat at a table with four other girls, all of whom were abnormally pretty and looked super confident. It was easy to guess that they were the coolest kids in the room. And guess what: Sailboat Girl was looking at me again. Was that a good sign—or a really bad one?

After lunch, the classes passed quickly. The final period of the day was history, where I was happy to learn we'd be covering Ancient Greece, a unit we'd just finished at Victoria Middle. Good thing, too, because Godzilla could have come stomping through the aisles and eaten three students and I wouldn't have noticed. I was too busy thinking about basketball. I was supposed to meet the team after school, and I *had* to make a good impression.

By the time the last bell rang, my nerves couldn't be ignored. I felt lightheaded as I walked to the sports center, pausing just outside the door to collect myself. Why was I being such a wimp? Sure, my scholarship at Lakeview hinged on a successful performance, but there was a reason they were recruiting me: Because I was good. No. More than good.

Raising my chin a millimeter, I strode through the double doors.

The court was empty except for Coach Ahmad. She was a small but sturdy looking woman, with dark brown hair pulled up in a loose ponytail, and eyes that seemed super focused, making her appear incredibly alert. She wore a decorative golden coin threaded onto a string around her neck, which she rubbed absentmindedly as she walked toward me— or, rather, limped. I had heard from Olive that Coach had permanently injured her left leg in a skiing accident a few years back.

"Word is that you have the skills to be our small forward," she said, her voice gruff.

The small forward was the team's most all-purpose player, with a balance of offensive and defensive capabilities. It had been my position at Victoria Middle.

"I think so," I said, trying to keep my voice strong.

"Although you did play for Victoria Middle," Coach Ahmad went on, as if I hadn't spoken. "They're our biggest rival, you know. Do I need to wonder where your loyalty lies?"

I shook my head vigorously. "No, Coach." I bit my bottom lip, wondering if my teammates would also question my trustworthiness. Then I had a brain wave. Rule 4: "Maintain Some Mystery!"

"But, um, maybe we don't need to mention to the team where I'm from," I said. Coach Ahmad raised her eyebrows, and I quickly tacked on, "At least not just yet. Let them get used to me first. I don't want them wondering the same thing you did."

Coach Ahmad looked thoughtful. "Not sure how well that will work. Someone might recognize you. But I won't say anything." She glanced up as a couple of girls emerged from the locker room. My eyes widened: One of them was Sailboat Girl. "Now go get changed."

She handed me a slip with my locker number and two jerseys, one for practice and one for games.

My game-day jersey was number 17. Acceptable—nothing symbolic to me, but it didn't have one of my bad luck numbers, like 6 or 4, either.

I changed quickly, trying to control my heartbeat, which kept speeding up. After pulling my hair back in a pony-tail, I joined the rest of the girls on the court. I studied them as they did warm-up drills. I didn't remember any of them from the game I had played against them last year. I could only hope they didn't remember me.

Half the girls did jumping jacks while the other half worked on lunges. I joined the lunging side. Sailboat Girl gave me a nod and a smile, and Olive waved enthusiastically, which seemed like a good start.

We switched over to squats and then to full-court sprints. I was just starting to break a sweat when Coach Ahmad blew her whistle. The team formed a semi-circle around her.

"Girls, this is Pippa Park," Coach said, jerking her chin in my direction. "She's a new student and, I'm told, a killer small forward."

By this point in the day, I was almost used to the appraising glances, yet one girl in particular made me self-conscious: She locked her grey eyes onto me with an aloof, judgmental gaze that made me want to wilt. However, the more she stared, the more familiar she looked. I tilted my head. Of course! She'd been in the game last year. If my memory was correct, she'd scored two three-pointers.

Coach Ahmad introduced us. "This is Bianca Davis. She and Caroline Bingham are co-captains of the team."

Caroline, a tall, willowy girl with thick auburn hair that she wore half up, half down, gave me a wave and a smile.

Bianca gave me a lukewarm nod. Coach Ahmad announced that we were going to do a shortened scrimmage, with no coaching from the sidelines. She didn't say it out loud, but I knew she'd be watching me the whole time.

After Coach brought out red and blue jerseys, she rattled off the names of the players. Team Red: Bianca, Olive, Jordan, Venus, and Winona to start, with a girl named Sam on the sidelines. Team Blue: Helen (Sailboat Girl), Starsie, Kathy, Caroline, and me, along with Divya and Tally on the side.

As we gathered in the middle of the court, preparing for the jump ball, Olive edged closer to me. "Just because we're friends doesn't mean I'm gonna go easy on you," she said with a wink.

I cracked a smile. "Back at you."

Coach threw the basketball up into the air, and Caroline and Winona jumped up after it. Winona knocked the ball forward toward Bianca, who dribbled it down the court. Starsie sprinted after her a second too late, and Bianca managed a neat layup. The girl was clearly captain for a reason.

"Defense," Helen called as Starsie tossed the ball from out-of-bounds toward Kathy. "Man-on-man, I got Bianca!"

Olive was closest to me, and so I started guarding her. Although it had been a while since I had played a full-on game, the motions came back to me quickly. The ball went from Winona to Caroline to Winona to Olive—and then to me, as I stole it from Olive's hands and passed it to Helen. She took off down the court and nailed a two-pointer. The thrill of adrenaline that rushed through me almost made it feel like it was me who had scored.

From that point on, everything fell into place and I stopped being nervous. I didn't have to tell myself to block out Olive using my hips—I just did. And I didn't have to tell myself to move left to catch Caroline's pass—I just did. When I sank my first shot a couple minutes into the game, Coach Ahmad gave me an approving look that sent my confidence soaring.

By the time Coach called out sixty seconds left, we were down one point, with a score of 18-19. I wanted to win so badly that my hands were clenched into tight fists, but the opposite team had Bianca and Winona—both really strong players.

I glanced at Helen—it was our ball, and if we played this right, we could win the scrimmage. She dribbled the ball down the court until Bianca pressed her. Helen feinted to the left, and for one clear moment, she had the perfect shot.

"Pippa—heads up!"

I hip-checked Winona, who was guarding me, and caught Helen's pass. Two more defenders crowded around me. One of my other teammates, Divya, was open but I hesitated. She'd missed all her shots so far. If she missed this one, too, then we were done. I couldn't risk that.

Back-pedaling to the three-point line, I shouted, "Over here, Divya," pretended to pass the ball over to her—and instead shot it high, and watched it sink through the hoop.

Helen and I high-fived as the whistle blew. Once again, we gathered in a semicircle around Coach Ahmad. Bianca, who I'd suspected would hate to lose to the new girl, nodded at me, something like respect in her eyes. Divya, though, gave me a cold look. And Olive didn't smile, either. "You play rough," she muttered.

I didn't get a chance to reply before Coach Ahmad started speaking.

"Good work today," she told us. "But don't rest easy. The season opener is coming up, and we're not going to lose to Victoria Middle again this year. Not for the seventh time in a row, and not on my watch. As for you Pippa . . ." Coach Ahmad grinned at me. "Welcome to the team."

It would have been totally uncool to let out a yelp of joy, so I kept my mouth shut. I'd save the cheers for when I got home. For now, I grinned back at Coach.

"Go get some water, everyone. See you all back here tomorrow. This is going to be a *great* season."

As we jogged toward the locker room, I couldn't stop the rush of happiness that bubbled up in my chest.

Sure, I hadn't even glimpsed Eliot yet. And yes, Mrs. Rogers's class had already managed to confuse me. And fine, Olive seemed kind of mad at me.

But still: best first day ever.

10

THE HEADMASTER

My first week at Lakeview passed in a blur. I was busy catching up in my classes, and Mina needed extra help at the laundromat. And, of course, I had practice every day after school.

When Monday rolled around, I could hardly believe it was my second week there. I arrived at school a few minutes early and headed to my locker. As I passed through the halls, my gaze darted from blond head to blond head, searching for Eliot. Since he was in eighth grade, we didn't have any classes together. Still, about once a day, we passed each other in the hallways. He never actually talked to me during those times, but he had nodded at me on Thursday, which I thought was pretty good progress. Unfortunately, he had to cancel our tutoring session again last week, although this time he had at least sent me a text so I knew not to show up at his house.

I reached my locker, hung my backpack inside, grabbed my math book, and glanced down when my phone buzzed. A text from Buddy.

Full stock of frosted animal crackers @ my house. Movie after school tmw?

Before I could respond, my phone buzzed again.

We can even watch the Little Mermaid, if you want

I smiled. Even though everyone always assumed I liked *Mulan* the best ("You look just like her!"), *The Little Mermaid* was my all-time favorite Disney flick. I had seen it at least ten times and still burst into tears whenever King Triton trashed Ariel's treasure trove. Not that I would let anyone but Buddy know that.

"Pippa!" Olive's nasal squeal in my ear made me jump.

"One sec."

Busy tmw, I texted Buddy back, feeling guilty. On Saturday, I'd bowed out of our usual basketball game in the park because Mina wanted me to get a head start on my homework. On Sunday, I'd had chores at the laundromat. And tomorrow was Tuesday, which meant tutoring with Eliot. There was no way I would miss that, especially after two weeks of cancellations.

Before I could text **Sorry** to Buddy, Olive clutched my arm.

"Oh my god, I have to tell you! I heard Bianca and Helen talking about you after practice Friday."

I pocketed my phone. "Talking about me?" I repeated nervously.

"What were they saying?"

"Nothing bad." Olive reassured me. "In fact, Helen said that you had potential. And Bianca didn't even disagree!"

I felt a weird wave of elation. Although it was only a simple compliment, it felt like a huge victory somehow.

"It's a big deal, Pippa," Olive stressed, apparently taking my silence as nonchalance. "There's a reason Bianca and Helen are called the Royals."

"The Royals?"

"Yeah—it's the two of them, plus Starsie, Win, and Caroline. Everyone calls them the Royals because they rule the school. Haven't you seen those golden hair ties they all wear on their wrists? It's like, their thing. I don't want to get you too excited, but let me say this: Impressing Bianca takes work. In fact, it took me three weeks packing up all the scrimmage jerseys on the team last year before she even acknowledged me!" Olive squeezed my shoulder. "If they accept you, we could be in!"

"Wow," I said, not sure what to say to that.

Classical music played over the speakers, and Olive beamed at me.

"Well, see you at lunch."

I headed to Mrs. Rogers's classroom. The first thing I noticed when I walked through the door was that Helen had taken the seat next to my usual spot by the window. I hovered awkwardly in the middle of the classroom then forced myself to walk casually to my chair. I tried my best to play it cool, nodding at Helen as I flipped open my textbook.

"Rough practice Friday," I said.

Which was the truth. Coach Ahmad might be little, but she was tough. On Friday, she'd made us play a game where everyone took turns shooting from the free-throw line. For every shot missed, we had to run a lap, only stopping when the girl with the ball finally made one in. Halfway through, and I was sweating more than I ever had before.

"For serious. When Olive's turn came up, I thought my legs were going to fall off," Helen replied. "Whenever she takes a shot, her arms look like limp macaroni. Let's face it. That girl cannot shoot under pressure!"

I gave a small, guilty chuckle. Olive was easy to make fun of, with her hit-and-miss shots and overeager attitude, but I still felt bad. Not wanting to offend Helen, I made up for it with another longer chuckle. And then I stopped, before Helen assumed I was some kind of strange chuckling machine.

"I wanted to hug you when you made yours on the first try," Helen added, and I felt a happy tingle. "Where did you say you used to play?"

Uh-oh. My pulse skittered. "Oh, you know, I—" I stammered.

"Pippa, Helen," Mrs. Rogers broke in. "We're waiting. Save the conversation for later, please."

Sweet relief. Dutifully, I took out my pen and started scribbling down notes, my heart thumping. For once, math had actually saved me.

At the end of class, Helen zipped out of her seat to catch up with Bianca, who was beckoning to her from outside the classroom, so I didn't have to face any more uncomfortable questions. Right before lunch, though, she popped up next to me while I was fiddling with my locker.

"Hey." She smiled.

"Hey." I echoed weakly. Half of me was hoping we could have another conversation about basketball, while half of me was worried she'd ask me again where I used to play.

Before either of those happened, I saw Eliot heading in our direction. I was so flustered that my hand flapped around in a manic wave before I could stop myself. "Eliot! Are we on for tomorrow night?"

He looked startled. "Yeah," he said, not slowing down.

He turned the corner, and immediately Helen placed a firm hand on my shoulder. "You're going on a date with Eliot? Where? When? How? Tell me everything," she demanded.

I blinked, taken aback. "It's not a date," I replied with a blush. "It's a tutoring session. He's my math tutor."

"*Just* a tutoring session?"

My cheeks turned even redder. "I mean, I definitely wouldn't mind if it was a date."

But to my surprise, Helen scrunched up her nose. "Oh no. You're new here, Pippa, so let me give you some advice. That boy? I mean, he's cute and all, but he's a piece of beef jerky." At my blank stare, Helen added, "You know—a total jerk. People here think he walks on water, and he totally acts like it's true."

"He is a little aloof," I admitted. "But—"

"But those dreamy-go-easy baby blues," Helen finished for me, batting her long eyelashes. At my sheepish look, she laughed—she had a warm, buoyant kind of laugh that was impossible to resist, and after a moment I smiled.

"I get it. The heart wants what the heart wants and all that," she went on. "Unfortunately, he doesn't care. Oh, and also, half the hearts at this school want him, too," she added.

I turned my attention to shoving my books in my locker, hiding my stricken expression. *Of course* Eliot had tons of admirers. Why hadn't I thought of that before? No doubt most of them had their nails done every week and tossed their clothes out when they weren't in season anymore.

He would never be interested in someone like me. In fact, maybe I had gotten it all wrong—maybe he wasn't the one behind my scholarship at all. Though I couldn't think who else could have set it up . . . .

I shut my locker door and had just turned back around when I saw a tall, familiar man striding down the hall—and this time, there was no mistaking the man: It was definitely Mr. Haverford. Again?

"Pippa, Helen," said Mr. Haverford crisply, meeting both of our glances as he walked by.

Wait. He knew Helen, too?

"Morning, Headmaster Haverford," Helen replied.

I froze, my mouth forming a perfectly round O.

"Headmaster Haverford?"

"Yeah," she said, not seeming to notice my shock. "Didn't you know? It's not enough for him to have just the looks and the smarts." She placed her hand on her hips. "Eliot Haverford rules this school in *all* ways."

11

PROGRESS

The next day, I was still grappling with this new information. I felt surprised but happy. On the one hand, I wondered why Eliot hadn't told me his dad was also the headmaster. On the other hand, the fact that Mr. Haverford was the headmaster made it even harder to believe that Eliot wasn't behind my scholarship. I thought about the Haverfords' car, sitting by the court as I played ball with Buddy. I could just picture the father and son duo watching me together. Confirming my skills. In my imagination, Mr. Haverford turned to Eliot with an expression of awe. "You're right, son. Lakeview needs her."

"Pippa Park." The voice of Mr. Donoghue, my Earth Science teacher, boomed from the front of the room. "Are you paying attention?"

"What? Oh, yes, of course." I turned my eyes toward the chalkboard.

After class, I headed to the lunchroom. Jung-Hwa had packed another lunch for me today. But although I had smiled at the cute bento-style meal he had prepared, complete with rice shaped to form a teddy bear face—with dried seaweed, egg, and sliced radish for his eyes, nose, ears, and mouth—I hadn't taken it with me to school. Instead, I had pretended not to see it. I couldn't forget the way Olive had sneered at my lunch that first day. Pizza slices from the cafeteria were safer. I might have to keep skipping sundaes with Buddy, though, so I'd have the cash to cover lunch.

After grabbing a cup of water from the fountain, I started for Olive's table, as usual. Halfway there, someone took my elbow.

"There you are." Helen looped her arm through mine, steering me in the opposite direction. "I've been looking for you. Come with me."

I craned my neck around just in time to see Olive's flabbergasted expression, but before I could say anything, Helen was ushering me to the table of Royals. As we set down our trays, the four girls, already seated, glanced up, but none of them looked surprised to see me. Had Helen told them she'd be inviting me today?

"Pippa, meet the only people you need to care about." Helen winked. "You know them all from practice, of course. Starsie, Caroline, Winona—"

"Call me Win," Win interjected.

"And, of course, Bianca," Helen said.

Bianca's smile felt perfunctory, but it was still the friendliest expression I'd seen on her face.

"Hey." As I sank down next to Helen, I hoped nobody noticed my hands were shaking. Because even though I had been on the same team with these girls for almost two weeks, this felt different. A kind of invitation.

"So, where are you from, Pippa?" Win asked.

I took a shaky breath, but reminded myself to keep cool. After yesterday's conversation with Helen, I'd spent some time thinking about how to deal with this question.

"Well, I'm Korean, but I was born in Boston," I replied.

Across the table, Bianca tilted her head. "It's weird— you look familiar," she said, her glossy lips pursing. She had been picking at a plate she'd filled with lettuce from the salad bar, but now she set down her fork and glanced at Caroline. "Doesn't she?"

Caroline narrowed her eyes at me, and my palms started to sweat. *Please don't let them remember me.* Hiding my discomfort, I forced myself to smile as I shrugged.

"Oh! I know!" Starsie chimed in. "She looks like Selena Huang!"

"Stars, they look nothing alike." Win rolled her eyes. "Besides, Selena is Chinese."

I glanced gratefully at Win, who shot me a look that said *ignore her.*

"Only half. I think her mom is Korean," Starsie said, somewhat petulantly. She popped a tater-tot into her mouth and chewed. "Or maybe their family was just vacationing in Seoul last winter break. Whatever." Aiming her fork at me, she asked, "Where in Boston did you live? My cousins have a house in Back Bay, and I love visiting them. Boston is so cool. Why would you ever move?"

"Maybe because her family moved?" Win shook her head. "So why *did* your family move?" she asked, her eyebrow arched, punctuating her questions.

"Um, my mom had to go back to Korea, but my sister and her husband are here in Victoria," I said. Yes! So far, I hadn't lied once. Okay, I had left out some vital details, but was it my fault if the Royals just assumed things about me?

"Anyway," said Bianca. "It's weird for anyone to transfer into Lakeview so late. I'm surprised they let you in if you missed the normal deadlines."

"Yeah," Caroline agreed. "My brother's best friend missed the final application date by one week, and he had to go to public school."

Although Caroline's voice was mostly matter-of-fact, I couldn't miss the slight edge to the way she said *public school;* it confirmed that mentioning my past was *not* a good idea.

"So what's the story? How *did* you get in?" Bianca demanded.

"Maybe she's well connected," Helen said pointedly. She caught my eye and shot a glance over at the table of jocks that was helmed by Eliot Haverford.

I gulped. Was she going to ask about Eliot and me in front of the other Royals?

No. Instead she launched into a story about how her dad's boss had helped her cousin transfer schools in the final month of the semester, and the heat was off. I let out a mental sigh of relief.

"So," Caroline said, her eyes roving to the table of jocks then back to Bianca. "How are things with you-know-who?" She lowered her voice and waggled her eyebrows.

Bianca shook her head, but I could tell that she was secretly pleased with the question. She glanced over her shoulder at the cluster of guys, but it wasn't clear which guy was the "you-know-who," and I didn't dare ask.

"He hasn't asked me out—yet," she replied, nonchalantly. "But I'm not worried."

I could see why she wouldn't be. With her looks and

confidence, few boys would turn her down. As if to prove the point, Bianca flipped her lustrous chestnut-colored mane over her shoulder and applied another layer of Very Berry Lip Balm.

"What about you?" Bianca asked, raising her eyebrows at Caroline. "Any progress with that cutie from French?"

Caroline gave the golden hair tie around her wrist a frustrated tug. "Not yet."

"What about Todd Ackerman?" Starsie said with a smirk. "He has a maaaaajor crush on Caroline," she explained to me. At the sharp look Caroline shot her, she giggled.

"He's a chess geek," Caroline said, rolling her eyes.

"Aw, but he's adorable!" Starsie teased.

"The same way a slobbery golden retriever is."

"Anyway, isn't he a scholarship student?" Bianca asked.

Her tone was mild, but Win's face suddenly went stiff and Helen looked down at her plate.

"Not that there's anything wrong with that," Bianca added quickly. "But . . . I mean, how would he even pay to take her on a date?"

I stuffed another bite of pizza into my mouth, trying to cover my panic and dismay. Another reminder that I should keep my home life very private.

"Enough about Todd Ackerman," Win said. She rolled her eyes. "Do any of you know how to talk about anything but boys?"

"What else is there to talk about?" Starsie retorted. She tilted her head at me. "What about you? Any cuties catch your eye yet?"

I hastily swallowed my pizza, caught in a moment of indecision. I didn't want rumors to get back to Eliot that I was mooning over him, but I did want to be part of the boy talk.

"Well, there is this one guy who's pretty cute," I admitted. "He—"

"Oh!" Starsie squealed as Helen knocked her water bottle over. I barely jumped up in time to dodge the worst of the spill.

"My bad," Helen apologized, passing me a wad of napkins.

I hadn't finished mopping up when the chords of Mozart announced the end of lunch, and the girls began to gather their things. Maybe it was for the best.

As we walked out of the cafeteria, Helen smiled at me. "I'm glad you sat with us today."

"Yeah, it was good to finally talk to you," said Win.

"And don't forget, we totally rescued you from Olive," Starsie chimed in, making Caroline smirk.

"See you at practice," Bianca added.

I waved goodbye to them, feeling giddy. I was trying to keep myself from getting too excited, but this was a big deal, and I knew it. Not only had I been invited to sit with the Royals, I had made it through an entire lunch period and they seemed to like me! For now, at least. But a sudden pang of nerves made my stomach cramp. What would happen if they found out about the real me?

12

THE MYSTERIES OF THE HAVERFORD HOME

Despite the cool weather, I was sweating when I showed up at Eliot's house. Basketball practice had run late again: Coach Ahmad seemed to like nothing more than to watch us sprint from one side of the court to the other as she lounged against the wall. Afterward, I'd changed my clothes and jogged all the way to the Haverfords to avoid being late.

I opened the front gate and walked through the weedy yard. Dry autumn leaves piled up in drifts, whirling in the chilly wind. The Haverford house, with its unkempt yard, round tower, and dark curtains drawn tightly over the windows, looked like a classic witch's dwelling.

I hastily checked my appearance using my phone's camera before reaching for the lion's head knocker. Hopefully, Eliot appreciated the flushed look. At least I didn't have any BO.

The locks turned on the other side of the door, and Eliot pulled it open.

On my way over, I'd decided that since the Rules of Cool seemed to be working with the Royals, I'd try applying them with Eliot. I was going to act confident, and if he tried to shut me down, I was just going to let it roll off me. One way or the other, we were going to have an actual conversation.

"Hey," I said sunnily.

"Hey," he said. His bored monotone didn't go with his eyes, which today combined the most dazzling shades of seafoam green and sky blue. *Don't stare so much*, I had to remind myself. *You want cool vibes, not stalker ones.*

"So," I said, as I followed him to the dining room. "I didn't realize your dad was the headmaster of Lakeview!"

Eliot didn't respond. But I kept going.

"That must be weird. Like, do you call him Dad when you're at school?"

I'd meant this jokingly but to my surprise, Eliot snorted. "Are you kidding? He'd flip. He acts pretty much like a headmaster whether we're at school or at home."

Whoa. Evidently, I'd touched a nerve. On the upside, at least Eliot was finally talking to me.

"It's always 'go, go, go' with him," he continued. "Get the best grades, study hard, work hard, practice hard." He inhaled deeply then averted his gaze, as if he hadn't meant to share that much. Sitting down, he flipped open his notebook. "Anyway, let's start—"

"I totally get what you're saying," I broke in quickly, hoping to keep the conversation going. "I'm pretty sure my family decided I was going to become an engineer when I was still in the womb."

He gave me an astonished look. "*You* want to be an engineer?"

"Well, no. I think you have to have at least a little talent in math to do that." I gestured helplessly at my textbook. "So that takes me out of the running."

Eliot chuckled.

Underneath the table, I gave a tiny fist pump. Laugh number four!

"Your family has your best interests at heart, young lady."

I whipped around to find Miss Haverford standing behind me. She wore the same evening gown and shawl as the last time I'd seen her. When I first met her, I found it strange how dressed up she'd been for late afternoon, but I figured she was going someplace and had to get a head start. Now I knew she was just kinda weird. At this distance, I could smell a faint musty odor rising from the cloth.

Once again, she eyed me as though I were something she'd found on the bottom of her shoe. "Are you my nephew's girlfriend?"

I choked, my face flaming. "Uh, no—" I coughed.

I glanced back at Eliot and saw that he'd gone completely stone-faced.

"Aunt Evelyn," he said. "You remember Pippa. I'm her math tutor."

"Oh, yes." Miss Haverford stared at me for another moment. Then, abruptly, her manner changed.

"Eliot, have you offered your guest anything to drink? Water, tea?"

"Oh, I'm not thir—" I started to say, but Miss Haverford waved her hand to cut me off.

"The poor thing is choking! I'm sure she'd like a cup of tea. So would I."

Eliot stood up. "I'll be right back," he said in a flat voice, before stomping off down the hallway.

I looked after him helplessly, then back at Miss Haverford, then down at my notebook, like that might make this situation less unpleasant. After a moment, Miss Haverford took Eliot's seat.

"Are you a fan of my nephew?" she questioned.

I shifted uncomfortably in my chair. How was I supposed to answer that?

"He's a handsome boy, isn't he?" she said musingly. "And he's terribly bright. Athletic, too." Leaning forward, she tapped the table with a long, yellowish fingernail. "But do you know what he is above all?"

I shook my head, hoping Eliot would get back soon with the tea.

"He's a *Haverford*," Eliot's great-aunt announced. She arched an eyebrow at me and nodded, as if she'd just clinched her argument.

"Right," I said, mystified.

"Being a Haverford means something," Miss Haverford went on. "Every member of this family has a position to uphold. Someone like Eliot has obligations—serious obligations. Do you understand?"

"Someone like Eliot"? I did not, in fact, totally understand what she was talking about, but one thing I heard loud and clear. I felt my cheeks start to heat up again, this time with anger as much as embarrassment.

Eliot's great-aunt was telling me that Eliot Haverford was too good for me.

13

WHEN TWO WORLDS COLLIDE

Mrs. Rogers smiled at me as she handed me my math quiz. "Not bad," she said.

I stared down at the grade written in red ink: B. "Yes!" I whispered. I might not have made much—okay, any—progress earning Eliot's affection, but at least tutoring seemed to be working. I carefully tucked the quiz into my math folder. Mina would be pleased. Maybe it wasn't the A+ she wanted, but I was only a few weeks into Lakeview and already showing improvement.

My whole look had improved, too, now that I'd started following some of the advice from *Tween Things*. I had tried out a new hair tip this morning. Thanks to a dab of coconut oil, my locks were super shiny. As we walked out of lunch, Bianca shot me an approving look.

"Your hair looks great today, Pippa," she said.

"Really?" I flushed then quickly straightened my

shoulders. I didn't want to appear too needy. It was hard to keep up the facade of confidence, but it seemed to be working. "Thanks. I decided to try something new."

"Well, it's working," Bianca said. "See you at practice."

She smiled at me as she strutted to class. In a pleasant daze, I turned and nearly ran into a boy from math, Kendrick Green.

"Oops! Sorry, Pippa, my bad," he apologized, swerving out of my way. We had never spoken before, but apparently he knew my name.

"No problem," I murmured, staring after him. I'd noticed something strange but awesome: After less than a week eating lunch with the Royals, the other kids were already treating me like someone who mattered.

"Today, we'll be working in pairs, taking a look at some of the major themes of *Pride and Prejudice* and examining the different paths the characters follow," Mr. Douglas announced as I hurried into English.

Immediately, everyone began to scan the room, searching for a partner to work with. I felt a pang of nerves. Who could I pair up with?

"No need to worry, I've already made the assignments," Mr. Douglas said.

A few of the kids groaned, but Mr. Douglas ignored them as he began to rattle off names, ending with . . .

". . . Tricia and George, and finally, Pippa and Divya."

I winced. I might be in with the Royals, but that didn't matter to Divya. She plain didn't like me. In English class, she rolled her eyes every time I spoke, and in basketball practice, she pretended not to see me whenever I was open for a pass. It took me venting to Helen at lunch to discover that Divya had hoped to be the starting small forward this year. She thought I'd stolen her position, even though I had nothing to do with it. I felt kind of bad but really, it had been the coach's decision.

Divya made no move to change seats. Feeling awkward, I gathered up my stuff and moved over to her. Arms folded, she stared at me with an air of disgust.

"Hi, Divya," I said, trying to sound cheerful. I searched for something neutral to talk about. "I like your hairclip. It's so colorful."

Divya sighed loudly. "Let's just get this over with," she said. "What do you think the most important themes are? Assuming you read the book."

I gnawed on the inside of my cheek. "Look, maybe we got off on the wrong foot," I said. "I didn't mean to take your spot on the team. I didn't even know you wanted to be small forward."

"Who told you that?" Divya asked, her lips tightening.

"Well, Helen said—"

"I should have guessed," she interrupted. "You think

you're hot stuff, hanging around with the Royals, making fun of anybody who doesn't have their own credit card."

"I don't—" I started, but she cut me off again.

"Well, I wouldn't get too comfortable if I were you. Bianca likes new things, but she gets bored fast. And Caroline might smile to your face, but that's *only* to your face. When you mess up, they'll drop you like a used tissue."

Turning in her seat so that her back was to me, Divya opened her notebook and began to write.

I sat there, stunned. Tears pricked my eyes, and I had to blink fast before they spilled over. I'd never had someone dislike me so much.

And what did she mean "When you mess up . . . "? Was that some kind of warning? Did she know something about my real life?

She doesn't know anything. She's just trying to shake me up. I tried to calm myself. But I could already feel my new-found confidence starting to fizzle . . . .

. . .

At the start of practice, Coach Ahmad blew her whistle and announced a scrimmage. Since Bianca and Caroline were the co-captains, they got to choose their teams.

"Caroline, first pick is yours," Coach Ahmad said.

108

My stomach flip-flopped uneasily. As the newest girl on the Jaguars, I'd probably be the last one standing. After all, when people like Bianca and Caroline chose teammates, skills were only part of the deciding factor; every team selection was also a display of favoritism. Still, there was nothing to do but stand tall, keep calm, and get through it.

First, Caroline motioned Win over. Bianca quickly claimed Helen, and then Caroline snatched up Jordan. I looked down at my shoes, expecting Bianca to choose Starsie next.

Instead, she called, "Pippa!" Helen gave me a fist bump as I joined the three of them. Caroline picked Starsie next, then Bianca chose Venus; Divya and Kathy went to Caroline; and Bianca took Sam and Tally. Finally, only Olive was left. Smiling tightly, she trudged over to Caroline's side.

"Guess this is my team," she said.

I tried to catch her eye and give her a smile, but she ignored me. I sighed quietly. When I switched lunch tables, it was clear from the way she kept making faces and thumbs up at me that Olive was waiting for me to invite her to sit with the Royals. But how could I? I barely knew them myself.

After a few days, Olive stopped making faces. But now she always stood with Divya in the huddle, and she didn't swing by my locker before first period anymore. In the hallways, she practically sprinted past me, acting like Coach Ahmed was behind her, blowing the whistle to go faster.

I'll talk to her after practice, I resolved. *See if she wants to hang out or something.* In the meantime, though, I had to get through this game with Divya. She sounded livid earlier, and I expected her to play dirty. So I watched her carefully, waiting for her to come at me hard. But nothing happened. It turned out to be a pretty routine practice.

When we were done, I changed quickly, gathered my stuff, and lingered at the mirror, waiting till the locker room emptied out. Olive stood at her locker, stuffing her practice clothes into her bag. "How's it going?" I asked her.

She glanced up. "Fine," she said in a cold voice.

"Hey, I was wondering—"

"Pippa!" I heard Helen call my name. Olive scowled.

"—wondering if—"

"Piiippaaaa!" Starsie and Caroline sang together.

I turned. All of the Royals were crowded at the door of the locker room. "Are you coming or not?" Bianca asked.

I licked my lips as I turned back to Olive, who was looking at me with raised eyebrows.

"Let me just see what they want," I said. I hurried over to the group.

"We're going to Duo's," Helen said, looping her arm through mine. "You in? You know you want to!"

I did want to. But I could feel Olive's eyes burning into me from across the locker room. Also, I had told Mina I would be at the laundromat right after practice. Of course, I could just tell her I missed the bus. As for Olive . . .

"I'm in," I told Helen. "Um—should I ask Olive if she wants to join us?"

Immediately, I could tell that I had made a mistake. Bianca pursed her lips, Helen winced, and Caroline raised her eyebrows.

"Or maybe another time," I quickly added.

"There's no space in my dad's car," Bianca said. "We're squeezing, as it is."

Helen tightened her hold on me. Bianca grabbed my free arm so that I was between her and Helen, and we moved like an amoeba toward the door.

I could have looked back at Olive, but I didn't want to see her expression.

Outside, Bianca's dad was waiting in a shiny red Range Rover. "Hop in, girls!" he called.

I felt guilty about Olive, but I pushed it aside. It was just so awesome to be one of the glamorous six piling into that luxurious car. Bianca took the passenger seat, Caroline, Helen, and Starsie took the second row, while Win and I snagged the back. Sinking into my seat, I inhaled the scent of leather. The car even *smelled* fancy.

As we pulled out of the parking lot, Olive emerged from the gym, backpack slung over her shoulder. *I'll talk to her tomorrow*, I promised myself. The thought made it easier to ignore the uneasy stirring in my stomach.

"Hello, darling," Bianca's dad said, squeezing her shoulder with his free hand. "How was school?"

"The usual," Bianca breezily replied.

She looked like she might say more, but her dad had already returned to whatever conversation he was having via the wireless earpiece attached to his ear.

"B's dad is an exec of this huge advertising firm," Win murmured to me. "He works all the time, but they're crazy rich."

Did Win know the financial status of all the girls' families? I almost asked her what her parents did but stopped short. That question might make her ask about my family, and the last thing I wanted the Royals to know about was Mina's grungy laundromat or Jung-Hwa's job at the factory.

So instead, I didn't say anything at all.

Right after we'd claimed a booth in the back of Duo's Diner, Mr. Hine appeared at our table. "Orders!" he barked.

He impatiently tapped his foot as we put in our requests. I'd discreetly checked my pockets in the car and found four singles, so I wasn't worried about the money, though I'd have to figure out lunch for the rest of the week. Ordering a large vanilla ice cream with extra fudge appeared to be a misstep, though, considering Bianca got a plate of fruit ("*sans* the cottage cheese, thanks"), Caroline ordered hot tea with lemon, and Win only asked for water. Luckily, Helen and Starsie went in on chocolate chip pancakes, making me heave a silent sigh of relief at not being the only one with a major sweet tooth. To be on the safe side, though, I changed my order to a single scoop.

"So, the season opener against Victoria is coming up soon," Starsie said. "You worried, Pippa?"

As always, when the subject of Victoria Middle came up I felt a knot in my stomach. Sooner or later I was going to have to come clean. If nothing else, they'd figure it out on game day, since the Victoria Middle players would all know who I was. I wadded up a napkin and gave it a small squeeze, trying to keep calm. Maybe I was making a big deal over nothing. Maybe the Royals would be cool with my public-school past.

"Why would she worry?" Helen answered for me. "She's going to crush it."

"She'd better," said Caroline. "Starsie and Win graduate this year. It's their last chance to end Victoria's streak."

"We haven't won a game against them in seven years," Win explained. Of course, I already knew this, but I still tried to look surprised.

Just then, Mr. Hine dropped off our orders. He didn't stick around to ask if we needed anything else.

Bianca scowled. "If we don't beat Victoria Middle this year, I don't know what I'll do." She crossed her arms. "I mean, it doesn't just reflect poorly on us, it hurts the school's reputation, too. Plus, it's just *embarrassing*, isn't it?"

The rest of the girls nodded. I sat there, appetite gone. The knot in my stomach was back and bigger than ever. Bianca had just answered my question: The Royals would definitely *not* be cool with my public-school past. I cringed as I pictured her screaming, "You used to go to public school? You played for *their* team?"

"Finally!" said a familiar voice from behind me.

My stomach plummeted. *Buddy.*

All the Royals turned to look as Buddy slapped my shoulder. "I was starting to think you'd been abducted by aliens and forced to submit to a probe," he said. "You don't call, you don't text . . . . Where've you been?"

My pulse started hammering. What if he mentioned school, or the Victoria Middle basketball team, or the laundromat and my sad little apartment with Mina and Jung-Hwa?

"Hey, Buddy," I said weakly. "I didn't see you."

"I'm over there with Jack and Cici." Buddy waved toward a booth on the other side of the diner, where a couple of my old lunch mates sat, laughing at something on Jack's phone. Buddy had always been closer to them than I was.

"Who is this, Pippa?" Helen asked me, her gaze on Buddy.

"Yeah, introduce us to your . . . friend," Caroline added, with narrowed eyes and a tone a lot less warmer than Helen's had been.

"Oh, my bad," Buddy said, switching his attention from me to the rest of the group. "Buddy. Hi." He bobbed his head.

"I'm Helen," Helen said, giving him a dazzling smile.

Besides Helen, none of the girls bothered to introduce themselves. They did, however, survey Buddy with interest. And while I had never looked at him as anything other than, well, Buddy—my easy-going friend with a house stocked full of Goldfish crackers—for the first time I evaluated him like other girls might.

He had straight white teeth, a warm grin, and his dark hair was appealingly tousled. But I'd never noticed how much he slouched. And while it was normal for him to wear scuffed tennis shoes, off-brand jeans, and a plain, wrinkled navy T-shirt, for the first time it struck me as noticeably grimy.

"Mina and Jung-Hwa doing okay?" Buddy asked.

"Fine," I said, gulping.

I had to change the subject ASAP. Mercifully, just then, I noticed Mrs. Jecknell arriving at Buddy's table with a heaping plate of onion rings.

"Oh, look," I said. "Your food just arrived. You better go or Jack will eat it all."

Buddy gave me a weird glance but nodded.

"Yeah," he said. "Okay. See you around then, Pippa."

"Cool. Later."

Buddy wasn't even out of hearing distance when Bianca started dissing him. "Did you see that grubby shirt?" She shook her head. "I couldn't tell if those were ketchup or blood stains."

"Forget the shirt." Caroline pounced on me. "Who was that?"

"Yeah, he's cute!" Starsie chimed in. "You've been holding out on us!"

"Maybe Pippa has her eye on him," Bianca suggested.

"I do not!" I exclaimed, blushing.

"Look at those cheeks!" Bianca laughed. "Are you sure?"

"A hundred percent," I said fervently. I could never think of Buddy that way.

"I've never seen him before." Caroline frowned. "What school does he go to?"

Uh-oh.

"I'm not sure where he's from. We, um, we shoot baskets together sometimes," I said, skirting the question. My answer wasn't a complete lie—I didn't know the exact city where Buddy had been born—it just wasn't the whole truth.

"Hmm," Bianca said. "Good thing you're not into him.

Those stains . . . " She trailed off, wrinkling her nose.

"That's not fair," Helen objected. "I agree with Starsie, he's cute. Do you know what grade he's in, Pippa?"

"Seventh, I think."

"Oh, that's part of the problem," Bianca said. "I'm more into eighth graders."

Win rolled her eyes. "Not *all* eighth graders," she said. "Just one."

Bianca clasped one hand to her chest. "What can I say? Eliot's just kind of perfect."

I felt as if someone had struck me in the chest with a sledgehammer. "Eliot Haverford?" I blurted, before I could stop myself. Everyone looked at me in surprise. Bianca's eyes narrowed.

"Pippa goes to Eliot for help with math," Helen explained.

"Really." Bianca's tone was silky.

"He's an amazing tutor," I said. Uh-oh, that sounded like I was gushing, although I hadn't intended it to. Bianca's expression grew suspicious. "But it's not like I'm into him or anything," I added hastily. Great, now I sounded defensive. "He's nice," I finished lamely, sticking my spoon into my mouth to shut myself up.

After an abnormally long beat, Bianca flipped her hair over her shoulder.

"Eliot is so charitable," she said cheerfully. "It's one of the things I like about him. Of course, you should squeeze in the tutoring *now*," she added, leaning in closer to me. And I might have imagined it, but I swear her irises darkened at least two shades. Then she leaned back against the booth. "Because once Eliot's my boyfriend? He won't have time for anyone but me."

14

THE PATH OF PIPPA PARK

"Ugh, my nail chipped during practice," Caroline said, inspecting a tiny fracture on her otherwise perfectly manicured forefinger.

"Mani-pedi night!" Starsie squealed, flinging her arms in the air.

I finished changing out of my practice uniform and turned around to see Bianca staring down at her own immaculate nails with an appraising expression. "I'm tired of this color, anyway," she said. "I look better in greens."

I was tired, too. But it had nothing to do with nail polish. It was a few days after Duo's Diner, and I still hadn't gotten over my tense conversation with Bianca or the whole Buddy encounter. Add keeping up with the Royals, managing my usual duties at the laundromat, basketball practice, and Lakeview's heavy homework load, and you got one flat-out, exhausted Pippa.

"It's settled," Starsie said. "Let's go to Moonlight Spa. They have those amazing massage chairs."

"Massage chairs do sound nice after that practice," Helen said, cracking her neck with a wince. "You in, Win?"

"I have to babysit my sister," Win replied, zipping up her backpack. "Don't go too wild without me."

"Can't make any promises. What about you, Pips?" Helen asked.

I was already in trouble with Mina for being late to the laundromat earlier that week. And I didn't have any money.

"Um, I've got a lot of homework," I began.

Starsie hooted. "Homework? It's Friday night!" Grabbing my hand, she studied my ragged, polish-free nails. "And, no offense, you definitely *need* a manicure."

"Yeah," Caroline chimed in. "That's not a good look, Pippa. You really should come with us."

Oh boy. I was starting to get used to the clenched knot in my stomach by now. I tried to sound casual as I asked, "How much do they cost?"

"I don't know, like twenty?" Bianca said, as though the price was nothing. "I mean, for just a basic manicure."

"Oh." The knot tightened a notch.

"Problem?" Caroline tilted her head at me, and I quickly focused on buttoning up my blazer.

"I just don't have that much cash on me," I said. "And I, uh, left my debit card at home."

"Don't worry about it," Helen said, wrapping her arm around my shoulders. "I got you. Just pay me back later."

I thanked her as we headed out, but inside, I was furiously calculating how many hours I would have to work at the Lucky Laundromat just to be able to pay Helen back. If a manicure was twenty dollars, then how many pounds of laundry was that? I closed my eyes, struggling to do the math. Two hundred. That was almost as heavy as Jung-Hwa!

I knew Mina would argue with me if I told her I was going out with my friends, so instead I just texted her and quickly stuck my phone in the pocket of my backpack. A few minutes later it chimed once . . . twice . . . three times . . . four times, announcing a slew of messages, but I ignored it.

Starsie's mom dropped us off at the salon, which was located a couple blocks west of the Alder Bridge.

"Twenty dollars for the basic manicure, thirty with shellac polish," the receptionist told us as we went in. "A combo mani-pedi is forty, sixty with the shellac."

"We'll have five combos," Caroline said carelessly.

"Uh, I just want a manicure," I quickly interjected. "A basic one."

"You sure?" Starsie asked. "Shellac is supposed to be super good for your nails."

I shrugged nervously. If only they knew how much of my future free time I was sacrificing just to be here. Free time that I didn't really have . . . .

"My favorite polish only comes in regular," I lied.

"Ooh, really? Which one?"

My eyes widened. Now I needed a new favorite polish. Which ones even came in shellac?

"Don't tell me it's Light Me Up Lavender," Starsie said. She pointed to a bottle of sparkly lilac-colored polish.

"Yep," I said, exhaling a tiny sigh of relief. I plucked the color from the shelf. "That's it."

"That was my favorite color for, like, a whole month," Starsie said.

"Right this way," the receptionist said, gesturing toward a group of five chairs.

Since everyone except me was getting a pedicure, I got to sit in the massage chairs, too. I vibrated gently, trying to hold still as my manicurist did something to my cuticles with a sharp metal device. I'd never been to a nail salon before. I was surprised at how much everything tickled.

"Sometimes I wonder what the point is of getting our nails done," Helen said, pulling a face. "They're just going to get chipped by the end of next practice."

I looked at my left hand, which was almost finished. Luckily, Starsie's old favorite color was, indeed, pretty.

"I'll make sure to enjoy it for the next forty-eight hours," I said.

"I like your optimism," Helen said with a warm smile.

I smiled back. Helen had a way of making me feel like I really did belong with these girls. Afterward, we exited Moonlight Spa as a group, our arms linked. As we stepped onto the sidewalk, Bianca gasped.

"Eliot!"

At Eliot's name, my head snapped up. There he was, walking toward us, with two other guys, a tall dude with a buzz cut and a stocky redhead. They were all wearing T-shirts and basketball shorts, and the tall one dribbled a ball. Eliot's golden hair was ruffled and his cheeks were flushed. *Nobody should be able to look as cute as him.* It was unfair.

Bianca stepped forward as they approached us. Without thinking, I did, too.

There was no mistaking the annoyance in Bianca's gaze when she saw that I had trailed along. With alarm, I noticed the rest of the group had stayed back. Should I back off? No. Too late now. It would be super-awkward. Besides, a defiant voice said in my head, I liked Eliot, too, so why should I make it easy for Bianca?

"What's up, Bianca?" Eliot asked. He glanced at me. "Pippa."

"Hey," was all I could manage.

"I heard you're a math whiz." Bianca twirled a strand of her hair around her pointer finger. "I was hoping you could help me with my homework sometime."

My mouth almost fell open. What a lame line. Buzz-cut and the other kid smirked at each other, so I knew they thought the same thing I did. But Bianca just batted her eyelashes.

"Oh." Eliot sounded surprised. But when Bianca gave him her most radiant smile, he shrugged and gave a half-smile. "Yeah, sure."

"Great," Bianca said. "I'll text you."

As she turned, she gave me a tiny, snarky grin. "Did you want something, Pippa?"

I couldn't even answer. I took a step back, a roaring sound in my ears. I'd made a huge mistake. Bianca was so much better at this than I was. I was just making an idiot of myself—and for nothing. Eliot had zero interest in me, and now Bianca hated me.

I followed her back to the other girls, my chest feeling hot.

"So?" Caroline demanded.

Bianca smirked. "I'm going to text him."

Starsie and Caroline both let out squeals. Helen high-fived Bianca, but I could feel her gaze on me as I stared at my shoes.

A red Range Rover drew up and Bianca flipped her

hair over her shoulder. "There's my ride," she chirped. She climbed into the passenger seat of her father's car. "See you all later."

The red car sped away, and Caroline whirled on me.

"What were you trying to do?" she demanded.

"Nothing," I said shakily. "I just—I just know Eliot, that's all."

"Tell us everything! What did you say? What did he say? What did Bianca say?" Starsie badgered me. "I can tell by your expression that *something* happened."

"You do look a little sick," Caroline agreed. She arched an eyebrow at me. "Or maybe you're always this washed-out."

The insult took a second to register. When it did, my throat felt heavy.

"*Caroline*," Helen reprimanded her.

"What? She does look pale."

Helen looked like she might say something else, but before she could, Starsie's mom arrived, and both Starsie and Caroline, who were neighbors, climbed into the car.

"I'm sorry about that," Helen told me, once we were alone. "Are you okay?"

"Don't worry about it," I said miserably. "It was nothing."

I don't think Helen believed me, but a black Acura pulled up before she could press me.

"You need a ride?" she asked.

I shook my head. "My sister should be here in a few minutes," I said. A lie, of course. No way would I ask Mina or Jung-Hwa to pick me up and risk the girls seeing our bruised apple of a car, with its ugly dents and scratched paint job.

I waved goodbye to Helen and then made my way home.

When I walked in, Mina was at the table, sorting through mail, while Jung-Hwa poured leftover soup into a large Tupperware container.

"There she is," Jung-Hwa called cheerfully.

He set a bowl of *yukgaejang* on the table and handed me a spoon. I pulled out a chair, and the noise made Mina flinch. She set down a formal-looking letter from the electric company and glared at me. The dark circles underneath her eyes seemed more pronounced than usual.

"Where have you been?" she asked sharply.

"Hanging out with some of my new friends," I said. "I texted you."

"Yes, and I texted you back and told you to come home," Mina retorted. "I needed you at the laundromat."

"Sorry. My phone died," I mumbled. I didn't have the energy for a fight.

Mina's lips thinned. "You know, just because you go to a fancy private school doesn't mean you can forget about your family obligations."

"Family obligations." She sounded like old Miss Haverford. I let out a little snort.

"Did you just *snort* at me?" Mina demanded. Her eyes were like two lasers. "Is that what you're learning from your new friends? Because let me tell you—"

Suddenly I couldn't take it anymore. I shoved back my chair and stood up.

"I'm sorry. I didn't mean to snort, okay? I'm—I'm going to bed," I said.

Mina stopped mid-rant, her mouth still open. If I hadn't been so upset, it would have been funny. Behind her, Jung-Hwa stood wringing his hands.

I stepped into my room.

This week officially sucked. I'd lied to Mina about my phone dying; I'd probably hurt Buddy's feelings at Duo's; I owed Helen a small fortune; and I was pretty sure Bianca hated me now. What was I doing?

I closed my door, lay down on my bed, and cried myself to sleep.

. . .

Saturday morning, I still felt terrible. I had a headache and my eyes seemed permanently swollen from all the crying I'd done the night before.

More than anything, I wanted to get out on the court and shoot hoops with Buddy, but when I texted him to see if he was around, he didn't reply. I knew it—he *was* mad at me for blowing him off at Duo's. I'd have to figure out some way to make it up to him.

There was one bit of good news. Well, good and bad news. Bianca sent a group text saying she had plans with Eliot for Sunday afternoon. Since she included me on the text, I had to assume she'd forgiven me for my dork-like behavior last night. Maybe I wasn't going to be a friendless outcast after all.

The bad news: Bianca had a date with Eliot.

I tried not to let it get me down. After all, it wasn't like I had much of a chance with him, even if Bianca hadn't been in the picture. Still, it hurt to think about the two of them together. I had to force myself to send an appropriately excited response, with some clapping emojis and hearts.

At breakfast, I asked Mina if I could put in extra hours at the laundromat. I had figured out that if I worked six hours today and tomorrow, I could make up a good chunk of the twenty dollars that I owed Helen. Not that I was going to tell Mina about that. It would only give her more things to criticize me for. "And I can do two hours every afternoon this week, too," I suggested.

"Out of the goodness of your heart?" Mina asked sarcastically.

I bit back a snarky answer. "I'm, um, kind of low on cash."

"We buy your groceries and your clothes," Mina said. "What do you need more money for? Besides, you struggle with your grades as it is. I don't think you can handle more responsibilities."

"My grades have been getting better," I said, trying to de-escalate the situation.

Mina shot me a skeptical look. I reached for my backpack and whipped out the now-crinkled math quiz from a few days ago. I placed the piece of paper with the red B written on the top into Mina's hands, trying not to look too smug.

She glanced down at the test, her expression unreadable as she tucked a tendril of her short, choppy hair back behind her ear, her lips pursing.

"Keep studying hard, and you'll get an A," she said, handing back the sheet. "If your GPA dips, you know what will happen."

I should have realized that Mina wouldn't be satisfied with the B. But I couldn't stop the disappointment that flooded through me, making my throat constrict. I shoved the paper back into my bag and looked down at my tofu omelet. A little bit of me wanted to strive harder so that I could bring Mina that A and watch the surprise flash through her judgmental eyes. But the biggest part of me thought: *She should be happy for me now. She should acknowledge my hard work.* Only, I knew that to Mina, an A wasn't something exceptional—it was just something expected.

Jung-Hwa cleared his throat. "Chuseok is next weekend," he reminded us.

"Oh," I said, perking up. "That's right."

Chuseok was like the Korean version of Thanksgiving, except the date moved around according to the lunar calendar. It was my favorite holiday—after all, who doesn't love eating oodles of *galbi, japchae,* and sweet rice cakes and then falling into a blissful food coma? Just thinking about the savory taste of tender bone-in galbi made my stomach growl. An endless amount of incredible food was just what I needed to cheer me up.

"Mrs. Lee is joining us, but we always have too many leftovers. You should invite Buddy, and maybe some of your new friends from Lakeview," Jung-Hwa suggested.

"I'll think about it," I lied. The vision of Bianca, Caroline, and the other girls trooping into our apartment made me break out in a cold sweat. First, Starsie would widen her eyes and claim that she didn't know apartments came this small. Then Caroline would complain that everything smelled like kimchi, and that her clothes were going to have to be laundered afterward—and that's not to mention what would happen if Mina offered to take her up on that. Bianca and Win—what would they say? I couldn't even bear to imagine it.

As the nicest of the bunch, Helen might try and stick up for me . . . but she would be judging me the entire time, too. How could she not?

"What is there to think about?" Jung-Hwa asked with his usual friendly grin. "Or don't they like to eat as much as you do?"

"Everyone is really busy," I lied.

"Well, tell them to clear their schedules," Mina told me. "I want to meet the people you spend all your time with."

I had a sudden image of Mina, laundromat owner, ordering Bianca to clear her schedule. I shuddered. Nope. No. Not a chance. They could never meet.

"Yeah, invite them," Jung-Hwa added. "We have to see if they're good enough to be friends with you." He reached forward to tap me on the nose, and I had to resist the urge to pull away. Oh god, imagine if Jung-Hwa tried to tap my nose in front of the girls? Bianca and Caroline would share *that* look.

"They're good enough, trust me," I said shortly.

My sister was studying me intently.

"I hope you're not becoming obsessed with the lifestyles of the rich and famous," she said. "That's the last thing we need in this house."

"What's so bad about being popular and having money?" I shot back. "Isn't that why you and Omma are always torturing me to do well?"

" 'Torturing'?" Mina repeated. Her nostrils flared as

I picked up my fork to start eating again. Mina's gaze locked onto the fresh coat of polish on my nails, and her cheeks hollowed, like she was sucking on something sour.

"Just hurry up and finish breakfast so we can start the dishwasher," she told me. "Or are those fancy fingernails of yours too good to load dishes?"

. . .

By Sunday afternoon I was so sick of the laundromat I thought I might scream, except that the only thing likely to come out of my mouth was dryer lint. I wanted to get outside, but the day was cold and rainy and besides, I had a mountain of homework. I should have started it the day before, but instead Jung-Hwa and I had binge-watched a bunch of episodes of some old Korean drama about a nun who has to pretend to be her twin brother and take his place in a band. It had seemed so worth it . . . at the time.

I sighed as I settled down on my bed to read *Pride and Prejudice*. I had to finish forty pages, with annotations, by Monday. Then I had to read about some dude named Solon for history, answer some questions for Earth Science, and practice writing sentences for French. And of course, I had plenty of math homework.

It was probably a mistake to try to do homework while lying in bed. My eyelids started to droop around the time Lydia eloped with Wickham in *Pride and Prejudice*. I perked up when my phone, which was lying on my pillow next to my head, vibrated with an incoming text. I hoped it was Buddy. Or Helen.

Or, of course, it might be Bianca letting us all know how spectacular her date with Eliot had been. I steeled myself and swiped to unlock the screen.

The message wasn't from Buddy, or Helen, or Bianca. In fact, it wasn't a text at all—it was a Facebook Messenger message from a user called *Throwaway74312*. The profile pic was simply a plain grey background, no photo. Bemused, I clicked on the message.

You might think you're Royalty, but you'll know better soon enough. Enjoy the ride, Pippa . . . but don't get too comfy. Soon everyone will learn about your lies.

My breath turned shallow and my back muscles locked up. What was—who was—*what did this mean?*

Which lies? Did someone know I'd come from Victoria Middle School? Did they know I was at Lakeview on a scholarship? Maybe they knew where I lived or saw me working in Mina's laundromat.

Who is this? I wrote back.

I waited. And waited. No answer.

Whoever Throwaway was, they obviously wanted to frighten me—and it was working.

15

THE RUMOR

The week passed in a whirlwind. I couldn't stop thinking about Throwaway. Who was it? What did they know? And when were they going to tell everyone?

All week I had kept stealing glances at all the faces in my classes, trying to decide if they knew some truth about me, and avoiding eye contact in case they did. It was impossible to concentrate on anything, even basketball practice. But it was Friday afternoon, and I hadn't heard anything more from them. *Maybe they're just bluffing*, I thought, trying to make myself feel better.

"Lower to the ground, Park! Bend those knees!"

Startled, I snapped back to the present—doing endless shuffles up and down the court. The first game of the season was coming up fast, and Coach wasn't letting us forget it. Every practice was an ordeal of painful drills: jogging up and down the court while dribbling two balls, performing infinite one-on-one defensive maneuvers, and practicing layups until my bones felt like lead and my muscles, like rubber. Today was no different.

Coach blew her whistle twice, and we transitioned into a scrimmage, but I couldn't relax into the game. My mind refused to focus on the court. As hard as I tried, I couldn't block Throwaway from my thoughts.

The first person who had popped into my mind was Divya. I kept hearing her say, "Don't get too comfortable." Just like the message from Throwaway. But when we'd been paired again in English class earlier that day, I'd managed to work a reference to Throwaway into our discussion about the characters in *Pride and Prejudice*.

"I don't think Lizzie meant to sound cruel to Charlotte," I said. "I think that was just a *throwaway* comment." I leaned on the word, my eyes on Divya. "Throwaway number 74312," I added, in case she'd missed the point.

I was hoping for some kind of guilty reaction, but Divya just rolled her eyes the same way she did at everything I said. "What are you talking about? Did you even do the reading?"

So maybe Throwaway wasn't Divya . . . .

"Defense, Pips!" Helen called, pulling me back into the scrimmage.

I hastily shifted left, forcing Olive backward. Letting out a huff, she passed the ball back to Kathy.

Could Olive be Throwaway? Did she resent me enough to have sent that horrible message?

"Rebound, Win! Block her out next time!" Coach blew her whistle. "Kathy, that's a double-dribble! Pippa, your ball."

Scowling, Kathy passed the ball to me, and I stiffened. Had that been simple competitive frustration in her gaze—or something more?

After sinking a two-pointer, I jogged over to get a drink using my shirt to wipe sweat from my neck. As I straightened from the water fountain, I sensed somebody behind me and turned around.

"Nice shot back there," Caroline complimented me.

I blinked. Caroline never said anything nice to me.

"Uh, thanks," I said.

I gave a quick smile and started back toward the court. Or tried to, anyway. Caroline shifted her stance so that she was planted firmly in front of me.

"So." Her tone said 'now that the formalities are over, let's get down to business.' "There's a rumor going around school."

"Not about me, I hope." I tried to keep composed, but internally I was shaking. *Here we go*, I thought, barely able to breathe.

"People are saying that you're, like, super into Eliot Haverford."

My eyes widened. *That* wasn't what I'd been expecting. In fact, in my stress over Throwaway, for the first time I'd almost forgotten about Eliot.

"Who told you that?" I asked. I forced my eyes to remain on Caroline—and not to flicker toward Helen, the only person I had actually talked to about Eliot. Helen was nicer to me than any of the other Royals. Could she be Throwaway? The possibility made me feel physically sick.

"Is it true?"

I flushed. Caroline had me pinned. I knew she would see through me if I didn't tell the truth.

But, I reminded myself, there were different ways to say the same thing . . . .

"I'm not going to deny that Eliot's cute," I said, choosing my words carefully. "It's a fact. But he's just my tutor."

I held my head high as Caroline scrutinized me. After a long moment, she shrugged.

"Good," she said, giving me a forceful pat on the back. "Keep it that way. Bianca gets possessive, and I wouldn't want you to land on her bad side."

Without waiting for a reply, Caroline jogged back to the court. She hadn't even pretended to take a drink of water. She veered off to find Bianca and, as I watched, whispered something in her ear. The two glanced over at me.

What were they saying? At least I could be reasonably sure it wasn't about my public-school past. I swallowed.

Not yet, anyway.

16

TRUE FRIENDS

"My arms feel like gummy worms," Helen groaned.

"Same. I almost collapsed trying to get my uniform off over my head," I complained. "My arms wouldn't lift past my shoulders."

As I waited for Helen to finish packing up her things, I rested my head against my locker. I was exhausted but somehow keyed up, too. Throwaway had me anxious enough—now the situation with Bianca and Caroline gave me more to worry about.

We walked toward the double doors of the sports center. "Wanna come watch a movie at my house to recover?" Helen asked.

I hesitated. On the one hand, the idea of hanging out with Helen, just the two of us, sounded great. It was Friday once again, so I could take a night off from homework. On the other hand, I had told Mina I'd work at the laundromat every day that week. If I bailed, she'd never let me forget it.

"Let me check with my sister," I said.

I quickly texted Mina, **OK if I go to my friend Helen's house for a while?** Maybe if I asked her instead of just telling her where I was, that would make her less likely to overreact.

A moment later Mina replied. **Thought you were working at Lucky tonight.**

I rolled my eyes. Then a second text came through.

OK but not for long. I can't come get you and I don't want you traveling after dark.

Grimacing, I tucked my phone away. "Okay, I can come, but only for an hour."

"Is it weird living with your sister instead of your mom?" Helen asked as we crossed the street.

"It bugs me that she acts like she is my mom. But I'm used to it by now," I replied.

Helen gave me a sidelong glance. "Really? But it's only been, like, a month since your mom went back to Korea, right?"

Oops. Dumb, dumb, dumb! I'd forgotten about that part of my story.

I gave a laugh that sounded fake to my ears. "I guess I adjust fast."

To my relief, Helen seemed to accept that answer.

"This is me," she said as she steered me up a walkway toward a two-story house of whitewashed brick.

Although not as impressive as the Haverford mansion, Helen's house was still five times bigger than my family's apartment. Her dad was in the kitchen when we walked inside, eating cereal and flipping through a book titled *Australopithecus afarensis: Ten Years of New Insights.*

"Hey, Dad," Helen said, grabbing us a couple of granola bars. "This is Pippa. We're going to hang out in my room."

Mr. Pelroy looked up from his reading and gave me a warm grin. He was a tall, balding man with square-rimmed glasses and strong laugh-lines surrounding his eyes.

"Ah, Pippa. Helen's told us about you. It's good to meet you," he said.

"You, too," I said as Helen took me by the hand and tugged me out of the kitchen. She had talked about me to her parents? What did she say?

I followed Helen upstairs to her bedroom, which was larger than mine and Mina's combined. In spite of the size, it felt cozy. The walls were painted a pale violet, and several lamps gave off a warm glow. A bed large enough for a family of five—with enough pillows and blankets for double that number—was the focal point. A big window with a window seat looked out on a shady backyard.

"Your dad seems nice," I said as we flopped onto the

mounds of pillows. I almost added, "especially compared to my sister" but shut my mouth before that could pop out. The less I said about Mina or Jung-Hwa, the fewer questions I would have to deal with in the long run.

"Yeah, both my parents are pretty great," Helen agreed. "We moved around a lot when I was younger, and so for a long time the only people we were close to were each other."

"Really? When did you move to Victoria?"

"In third grade," Helen said. "That's when Dad got a full professorship at Bartholomew College. My mom still travels a lot for work, which sucks, but it's better than having to switch cities every couple of years."

"Mmm." I hoped she didn't ask me about my own "move." Unwrapping my granola bar, I took a bite.

"Bianca was my first friend at Lakeview," Helen continued. "I met her during recess on my first day. There was a girls-against-boys basketball game and we creamed them. It was awesome." She grinned. Then, her smile fading, she added, "I know she might seem a little cold sometimes, but really, B's a good person. She's just kind of stressy. She freaks out when things don't go her way."

"I'm trying to picture Bianca freaking out," I said. "My mind is blank."

Helen giggled. "That's what I like about you, Pippa. You make me laugh."

There was a little silence. I licked my lips, trying to figure out how to bring up what was on my mind. Out of all the Royals, I liked Helen the most. She seemed so warm and genuine. But could I trust her?

I tucked a strand of hair behind my ear.

"You know, Caroline came up to me at the water fountain today," I said. I studied Helen's face, but she just looked expectant.

"And?"

"She told me that there's a rumor going around school," I said. Still no reaction. "That I'm really into Eliot."

"Oh." Helen blinked, her mouth popping open. She looked genuinely surprised.

"Yeah," I said. "Which was . . . um, weird. Because, you know. I haven't told many people . . . or, I mean anyone, besides—"

"Besides me," Helen finished. Her tone was steady, but there was a hurt look in her eyes.

I fell silent, already feeling guilty. "I'm sorry—" I started, but Helen cut me off.

"It's cool. I see why you might think that. But I promise you, I didn't tell anyone about that conversation. I wouldn't do something like that."

"I *am* sorry," I said again, and I meant it. A second ago, I had felt like I had no choice. I needed to ask her. I had to know. Only now, my distrust seemed terrible. Helen was a genuinely nice person. And the one person I believed truly liked me. "Sorry," I said again. "I shouldn't have even asked."

"It's okay," she assured me. "I get why you did."

"I just wish I could figure out where this rumor came from," I added.

Helen let out a snort of laughter then immediately looked apologetic. "Sorry. But honestly, Pips? After Duo's Diner, it was pretty obvious."

"Really?" I flushed. "I thought I covered for that."

Helen shook her head. "I wouldn't say you were subtle. And running after Bianca and Eliot like a lost puppy last week—no offense—that didn't help. I'm pretty sure Caroline and Bianca figured it out on their own. Maybe some other people did, too."

"Oooohhh," I moaned, pulling one of Helen's fuzzy blankets up over my head to hide my flaming cheeks. "Can I stay underneath here forever?"

"It'll be okay," Helen said, giving my shoulder a sympathetic pat. "The Royals can be kind of judgy, but we tend to have short attention spans. In a few days this will blow over, I promise. Bianca and Caroline will forget the whole thing."

Under the blanket, I closed my eyes. A few days? If Throwaway74312 really did know my secrets and the Royals found out about them, this would last much longer than that. More like forever.

When I didn't answer, Helen asked, "What are you doing tomorrow, by the way?"

I emerged from the blanket. "It's Chuseok," I told her. "Kind of like Korean Thanksgiving. We'll be cooking and eating all day."

"Oh, yum!" Helen exclaimed. "We lived near a Korean restaurant in Philadelphia. The food was so good. I love those sticky rice cakes coated in that sweet, spicy sauce."

"*Tteokbokki!* It's one of my favorites, too. We'll probably have them tomorrow."

"Mmm. I haven't had them in forever."

Helen gazed expectantly at me. I realized with a shock that she was hoping I'd invite her over.

I opened my mouth, but I couldn't do it. I wasn't ready for any of my Lakeview friends, not even Helen, to see what my life was really like. I needed more time.

"It's kind of a private family thing," I said lamely. "But I'll bring you some leftovers on Monday. No tteokbokki though. It's better when it's hot."

She looked disappointed. "Okay."

There was another short silence, this one awkward. I cleared my throat. "I should probably get going before my sister decides to roast *me*."

"That would be tragic. Especially because you wouldn't be able to bring me leftovers!"

We both laughed, but the easy feeling I'd had with Helen had passed.

I said goodbye to Helen's dad, declined his offer of a ride home, and headed to the bus stop in the October twilight. On the bus, I wondered how I had gotten myself into this mess. I hadn't exactly lied, but I hadn't corrected people's wrong ideas about me—and it was getting harder and harder to keep the truth hidden. And now Throwaway was threatening to reveal everything.

I'd wanted a different life, but changing myself into the popular, private school Pippa had left me feeling more alone than ever . . . .

17

FOMO

It was nearly noon, and the nutty scent of sesame oil and spicy gochujang drifting out of the kitchen made my mouth water. Mina and Jung-Hwa had been in chaotic Chuseok meal preparation mode all morning. I had offered to help them, but our tiny kitchen was cramped enough with two moving bodies, much less three.

Instead, I lay sprawled out on the living room couch. Mina had suggested that I work on some math problems, but I couldn't force myself to start. I hadn't received any more texts from Throwaway, but it was hard to concentrate on anything else. So I flipped idly through my battered copy of *Tween Things* magazine, pausing on an article called "Everything You Need to Know About Makeup."

I'd never been interested in makeup, but now I started thinking about it. Bianca wore mascara and lip gloss every day. So did Caroline. Maybe I should, too.

I tried to push away the hope that it would get Eliot to notice me. *This is not about Eliot,* I told myself. *It's just about trying new things.*

Heading into the bathroom, I grabbed Mina's make-up bag. For somebody who always stressed that popularity meant nothing, Mina sure did have a lot of cosmetics. I retreated to my room, where I sorted through pencils, palettes, and face masks to find the basics my magazine recommended: concealer, blush, eyeshadow, mascara, and lipstick. Propping open *Tween Things,* I flipped to the article on makeup. Apparently, you were supposed to use it to enhance, not to mask. "Less is more," the article advised.

With that in mind, I dabbed concealer on the inflamed pimple that had erupted at my hairline, covered my lids with pink eye shadow, layered on blush, and carefully outlined my lips with a brownish-red pencil. The mascara was the hardest part—I kept almost poking my eyeball out with the curved stick, and when I flinched, the mascara smudged below my eye, and I had to wipe it away and try again.

Afterward, I studied the result in the mirror. Although I had used a bit too much blush, I didn't look bad. In fact, maybe with more practice, I'd get as good as Bianca.

Eliot likes Bianca's look, a little inner voice said. *Her big grey eyes, her thick brown hair.*

I shook my head. *Don't think about it, Pippa.*

"Pippa!" Mina barged into my room. "I need you to go

to the grocer for—is that my eye shadow? And my lipstick? What are you doing?"

I cringed. "Nothing. I just wanted to try it on."

"Ask permission before touching my things! Besides, you're too young for makeup."

"Lots of girls in my class wear it. Anyway, I was just trying it," I repeated, my tone defensive. Wanting this conversation to be over, I quickly added, "What do you need from the store?"

Mina frowned, obviously debating whether to let me off the hook so easily. A beat passed, and she relented. "Jung-Hwa forgot to get shrimp for the *saeujeon*. I need you to go to David's Divinities to pick up half a pound. Also, I put a load in the washer downstairs. Transfer it to the dryer on your way out."

She slid her wallet from her pocket and handed me a ten. I tucked it in my pocket, pulled on my jacket, and started walking out of my bedroom when Mina grabbed me by the wrist.

"Not so fast," she said, pointing to the pile of makeup on my dresser before stomping back to the kitchen.

I rolled my eyes but piled everything back into the bag and returned it to the bathroom, pausing at the mirror to examine my newly made-up face. One thing was for sure: It didn't go with my outfit of threadbare jeans and an oversized T-shirt. The best thing about the Lakeview uniform was that I was never any more or less out of fashion than the other girls, but David's Divinities was one of the fancier grocery stores in town. What if I ran into one of the Royals while I was there?

I returned to my bedroom to riffle through my closet, trying hard to spot an item that had been bought this year and looked halfway decent. I narrowed my eyes at the selection, skipping from an oversized, and extremely hideous, red blouse to a white shirt with a faded mustard stain on the front.

Finally, I settled on the same dress I had worn to the Lakeview tour, this time paired with dark leggings and a brown jacket. I smiled at myself in the mirror, liking who I saw. Making sure to grab the money from my other pocket, I hurried out the door and marched my bike down the stairs.

I ducked into the Lucky Laundromat and checked on the washer. The cycle hadn't yet finished, and so for a minute, I stood in front of the machine, watching as the water slowly submerged all the clothes before flipping them upside down. This used to be one of my favorite things to do at the laundromat. It had always reminded me of an astronaut's helmet, reflecting back a colorful alien spacescape. Today, though, I was more interested in my own reflection. I traced the outline of my high cheekbones, wondering what other people saw when they looked at me, and whether or not they liked what they saw.

The washing machine dinged, and I popped open the door. As I dumped the wet clothes into the dryer, I wondered what I would do if Bianca or Caroline walked through the doors. Pretend I was just another customer? I would have to.

The thought made me hurry from the building and start for David's Divinities. Usually, Mina and Jung-Hwa did the shopping in bulk. There was a Korean supermarket in the next town with cheap prices and a huge selection, but it was too far without a car. David's Divinities, however, was just across the Alder Bridge. I pedaled over the span, squinting as the wind tossed gritty dust at me. "Ow!" I muttered as something lodged in my left eye. I rubbed at it, hoping it wasn't a bug or anything gross.

I parked my bike at the curb, not worried about thieves. Nobody would steal a rickety thing like that in a neighborhood like this. I applied a fresh coat of cherry Chap-Stick, smoothed out my dress, and went inside.

The aisles were stacked with gorgeous displays of cookies and candy, as well as free-sample stations. I stopped to try a piece of freshly cut mango and nearly shouted with joy, it tasted so silky and sweet. Normally, I would feel out of place in this shiny-floored wonderland, but today I thought I blended in pretty good and held my head high.

I got the shrimp from the seafood counter and was just starting through the produce aisle when I spotted the familiar shaggy blond hair of Eliot Haverford, who was piling yellow apples into a paper bag.

As always, my heartbeat went crazy. It flashed

through my mind that Bianca would be mad if she saw us together, but in that moment, I didn't care.

I continued down the produce aisle. When Eliot looked up and saw me, I pretended to be surprised.

"Pippa?"

"Oh, hi, Eliot," I said breezily.

He blinked. "You look . . . different," he said.

"Thanks," I said. He noticed!

Then he said, "I think you have some dirt under your eye." He pointed. "There."

"D-dirt?" I faltered. I swiped at my cheek with a finger. It came away with a black streak on it. Oh god. My mascara must have smeared when I rubbed my eye to get the dust out. How bad was it?

"Yeah, you got it," Eliot said. "Well, see you."

And he walked away.

For a moment, I couldn't force my feet to move. I stared after him, disappointed and baffled. Why had he bothered to get me into Lakeview when it was clear that he didn't have any interest in me? And why couldn't I just let this crush go?

On my way to the cash register, I checked my reflection in one of the glass beverage fridges. It was true that the mascara under my left eye was smudged, but only a little. So at least I hadn't looked like a raccoon.

Feeling slightly better, I rode back to the apartment

and hauled my bike upstairs. The second I opened the door, the mingled scents made my stomach growl. My mood rose another notch. Who could be gloomy on Chuseok?

In the kitchen, I plopped the shrimp onto the crowded counter and then squeezed in between Mina and Jung-Hwa, stealing bits of galbi from the japchae, popping *gimbap* into my mouth, and sniffing at the spicy tteokbokki bubbling on the stovetop.

While Jung-Hwa grilled pork belly, Mina stuffed rice cakes with a blend of ground-up, sweetened sesame seeds and set them aside to be steamed over a bed of fragrant pine needles. Next, she set out a bowl of perfect little walnut cakes filled with red bean paste. I reached over and managed to gobble two down before she shooed me away.

"Stop stealing food," she said. But she was smiling. Like I said: Who could be gloomy on Chuseok?

Gazing at all the delectables, I made a decision— Jung-Hwa and Mina were right: This much food was made to be shared. So I texted Buddy. Hopefully, he'd had time to get over being mad at me about Duo's.

Chuseok's today. Come over—there's loads of gimbap

I slipped the phone into the side pocket of my dress, but when I didn't feel a buzz after a few minutes, I opened up my Messenger app. The "seen" icon had popped up, but there was still no reply.

So maybe he hadn't quite forgiven me yet . . . .

Mrs. Lee arrived with Boz clutched in her arms. She climbed the short flight of stairs with lots of loud sighs then plopped down into a chair. I brought her a glass of water to help her recover.

"When are your new friends coming over?" Jung-Hwa asked me.

"Oh. Um, they're really busy," I said, feeling guilty.

"All of them?"

"Yeah. It was probably my fault. I didn't let them know early enough," I replied.

Mrs. Lee and Mina made some comments about how young people didn't have any sense of time, but Jung-Hwa peered over at me from the stove. I could tell he knew I was lying. Although, technically this wasn't a lie. I hadn't told them early enough because I hadn't told them *at all*.

"And Buddy?" Jung-Hwa asked.

"I guess he must be busy, too." I felt a pang. "He never answered my text."

"I see."

As I set out four plates, four spoons, four pairs of chopsticks, and four bowls, I dodged Jung-Hwa's inquisitive gaze. Luckily, once the pork belly had sizzled to a golden brown, and Mina had doled out rice and side dishes, his attention shifted to the food. Just like mine. And Mrs. Lee's. Our neighbor was elderly, but there was nothing frail about her appetite.

The food was so good, I didn't think about Throw-away, Buddy, Eliot, or Bianca once during dinner.

"This is delicious," Mrs. Lee said as she picked out a bit of sweet potato from her japchae and popped it into her mouth. "It reminds me of home." Setting down her chopsticks, she turned to Mina. "How is your mother, by the way?"

Mina sighed. "She says she's fine, but she always sounds tired. And she's lost a lot of weight. Of course, every time I push her to go to the doctor she takes it as an insult."

"Stubborn woman," Jung-Hwa said. He smiled. "It runs in the family."

After dinner, Jung-Hwa brought out a deck of Go-Stop cards. The cherry red cards were about a quarter of the size of traditional playing cards, and instead of numbers, each was decorated with its own design, from chrysanthemums bursting with color to delicate iries to falling maple leaves. Jung-Hwa shuffled and dealt the deck, and Mina doled out an even number of *Pocky*—chocolate-covered biscuit sticks—to each of us, except for Mrs. Lee, who preferred to observe. I looked down at the seven cards in my hand, which included two ribbons and two animal cards. Not bad. I put down three Pocky sticks. In this family, we gambled with sweets instead of actual money. Word was that our great-grandfather had lost four chickens in a high-stakes Go-Stop game long ago. Nowadays, we tended to be more cautious.

After four rounds, the game was interrupted by Mina's phone ringing.

She picked it up. "Happy Chuseok, Omma," she said, turning on her speaker phone just in time for me to hear my mom's tired voice echo the words back to us. She sounded half-asleep, probably because it was about six-thirty in the morning her time.

"Pippa, *eodiya?*"

"I'm right here, Omma," I said.

Even though I hadn't spoken to her in over a week, the first thing out of her mouth was, "How is school? *Seong-jeok-eun eotteoni*"?

"My grades? They're improving," I said. "And I'm doing great in basketball."

"*Dwicheojijima.*"

"I'm trying as hard as I can."

"Omma *silmangsikijima.*"

"I won't disappoint you," I said, my voice growing tetchier.

"Pippa? *Saranghae.*"

I sighed. "I love you too, Omma."

Mina took the phone off speaker and asked Omma if she had gone to her doctor's appointments last week. I could tell from her angry expression that the answer was *no*.

Jung-Hwa packed the Go-Stop cards back into their

case, and I helped him wash and put away the dishes. We worked in comfortable silence until Mina got off the phone with Omma, and then Mina, Jung-Hwa, and Mrs. Lee settled down in the living room to watch *My Girlfriend Is a Nine-Tailed Fox*, Mina's newest K-drama obsession.

I started to watch it with them, but they were in the middle of the season already, and after a while I got restless. It was weird. Before starting at Lakeview, I had never minded hanging at home. I was happy to spend my nights watching shows with Jung-Hwa or playing games online. But suddenly, sitting around on our threadbare sofa bored me. Since I'd become friends with Helen and the others, I felt haunted by the sense I was missing out on something fun somewhere.

I went into my room and sat on my bed. **Hey, you wanna do something tonight?** I texted Helen.

I hadn't even set down my phone when it buzzed with what I thought was her reply. But when I looked down I flinched.

It was from Throwaway74312.

Do you believe people really like you? I think they're just faking it. But then, you don't need me to tell you that . . . you know all about being fake, don't you?

(PS: check out the pics Bianca just posted. What are you doing tonight?)

Feeling slightly nauseated, I read the message again,

trying to process what was happening. This time, my eyes lingered on the phrase "faking it." I squeezed my eyes shut. Was Throwaway right? Did the Royals only fake-like me? I knew Bianca and Caroline did. But Win? Starsie? Even Helen?

My fingers twitched and even though I knew better, I clicked over to Bianca's Instagram page. The first thing that caught my eye was a photo uploaded just twenty minutes ago. Party at C's! the caption said.

The picture looked like an advertisement for a girly pajama party, featuring Helen, Bianca, Caroline, Win, and Starsie. They were cuddled together on a long sofa with a dozen furry throw pillows and matching polka dot pajama bottoms, their heads thrown back in laughter. They all looked one hundred percent happy and completely close. None of them looked like maybe they were missing me.

Why hadn't they invited me?

The thought was sharp and bitter, making everything hurt. My stomach churned uneasily.

My phone buzzed again, and the muscles in my back automatically tensed. But this time, it wasn't an anonymous message—it was Helen.

Srry, I'm at Caroline's. Thought you had that family thing?

I blinked down at the text, feeling stupid. I had for-

gotten that I'd told Helen about Chuseok. That probably explained why I hadn't been invited tonight.

My phone buzzed again and I looked down, hoping
maybe Helen was going to tell me that there was still time to
join. Instead, it was Buddy.

Just now saw this. Tell Mina + Jung-Hwa sorry

I frowned down at the screen. Didn't he know that he
had his "seen" reports on? I thought about calling him out on
that, but I didn't want to fight. Instead, I texted him:

We still have a lot of leftovers

I'm busy right now, he wrote.

Oh really? Doing what?

Something grubby

I tightened my grip on my phone. So he *had* overheard us talking about him at Duo's. Worse, he'd heard
Bianca's mean comment—and I hadn't even defended him.

A wave of shame hit me. I'd been ignoring him to
impress snobs like Eliot, who barely had time to acknowledge me, and Bianca, who was casually cruel. I closed my eyes.
Buddy was my best friend. He was the most loyal person I
knew, and without him, the last four years of my life would
have been miserable. His friendship meant more than I would
ever be able to tell him. But maybe it was too late for that. I
bowed my head.

Buddy refused to see me, and now my new so-called friends were hanging out without me. I felt like I had nobody left.

Trying not to cry, I wrapped my arms around myself. I had to fix things, but where to start?

18

CRISIS

"Pippa Park, would you stay a minute?"

I glanced up at Mrs. Rogers. Class was over, and all around me kids were packing up their things. Helen cast me an inquisitive glance, but I raised my shoulders; I wasn't sure what Mrs. Rogers wanted.

I'd gotten a B- on the last math quiz—that wasn't great, but it was a long way from failing. I hoped she wasn't going to lecture me about spacing out in class. Over the last six weeks, I hadn't received any new texts from Throwaway, but I kept waiting for something horrible to happen. That and Coach's intense practices had left me both distracted and exhausted.

After the last person left the room, I headed up to her desk.

"I was grading the homework from yesterday," she started. "But yours wasn't in the pile. Again."

"Oh," I said. "I'm sorry, I guess I forgot to hand it—"

"This is the second time since you joined my class," Mrs. Rogers broke in. "And your last quiz grade dipped, too."

I shifted uncomfortably from one foot to the other.

"Even now, your eyes are glazing over." Mrs. Rogers was starting to sound irritated. "Your head hasn't just been in the clouds lately. It's been all the way up in outer space. What's going on, Pippa?"

"I'm sorry," I said, trying to think quickly. "I guess I'm just nervous, with the big season opener around the corner. Coach really wants us to win."

Mrs. Rogers sighed.

"I can see how that would take away some of your focus, but I want to emphasize the fact that you've already forgotten to turn in two assignments. A third strike will seriously endanger your grade, which is the foundation on which your entire tenure at Lakeview rests. I'm sympathetic, Pippa, but I can't bend the rules for you."

I nodded unhappily. *I know.*

I tried to pay special attention during my next few classes but found it hard to concentrate. Our history teacher kept us for a few minutes after the last bell. When we finally escaped the classroom, one glance at my watch revealed I was running late for practice.

I quickly gathered my things and rushed to the locker room, but before I could even take off my blazer, Coach walked in and told me to stay in my school uniform. "You're wanted in the front office."

My heart thudded. "Why?"

"Knowing those kinds of things is above my pay grade," Coach said, her arms crossed. But when she saw my worried expression, she uncrossed them and shrugged. "I'm sure it's nothing terrible."

As I hurried to the office, Mrs. Rogers' words nagged at me, and the B- math test weighed heavier than a brick in my backpack. Had my GPA dipped below 3.0? I thought I had until the end of the semester to prove myself. Had Lakeview decided to toss me out already?

Then I pushed through the doors into the office and stopped short, not understanding what I was seeing.

"Jung-Hwa?"

Suddenly, all the panic drained from one side of my brain to the other. What was Jung-Hwa doing, standing inside the office?

He looked so out of place here, with his uncombed hair and his grimy blue factory coveralls. His expression was strained, and a thin sheen of sweat dotted his forehead. He was even carrying a plastic grocery bag with his regular clothes stuffed inside it. Who had seen him? If any of the Royals spotted me with him right now. . . .

"What are you doing here?" I asked, hurrying closer and peering up at his face.

"You have all your things?" he asked, ignoring my question.

"Yes, but Jung-Hwa, why are you here?" I repeated.

Taking my arm, he steered me past Ms. Elkington, the red-haired secretary. She nodded at him, her expression grave, and he nodded back silently.

Now my panic changed again, intensifying. *Something is very wrong.*

"Jung-Hwa? What happened? Please, tell me."

We went down the front steps and toward the parking lot. "I'm sorry, Pippa," he said at last. "Your mom was in a car crash."

At the phrase "car crash" everything in my line of vision seemed to blur.

"She's in the hospital, in critical condition."

I dug my fingernails into the palms of my hand. Omma? But she was so strong. Invincible.

"Critical condition? What does that mean? And where—how did the accident happen?" My voice rose anxiously with each question.

"I don't know any more than that. Mina is talking to the doctors right now."

"Jung-Hwa, is everything going to be all right?"

"It will be fine," Jung-Hwa said, but his eyes were fixed on the car door as he opened it for me, so I couldn't tell if he was lying or not.

Although Lakeview was only a ten-minute drive from the apartment, the distance felt like miles. I couldn't seem to force enough oxygen into my lungs. Every time I came close, my chest would ache and I'd have to let all the air out again.

"Mina will know more by now," Jung-Hwa said as he parked the car. The two of us hurried upstairs to find Mina standing in the living room, the phone pressed to her ear. When she saw us, she held up her finger.

"Yes, I understand," she said in Korean. "Yes. Yes. Thank you."

She hung up.

"Was that Omma?" I demanded.

Mina shook her head. "No, one of the doctors."

"What happened?"

"She ran a stoplight," Mina said, brushing a hand over her tired face. "Another car slammed right into her. After it hit the passenger side, her car spun out of control, and she had a head-on collision with a light pole."

Tears welled in my eyes. "Is she going to be okay?"

"She's in surgery right now." Mina's voice was ragged. "The doctors couldn't tell me anything definitive, but they say she'll live." She glanced around her in a distracted way. "I booked a flight that leaves from Boston late tonight. What am I forgetting to do?"

For the first time, I registered the open suitcase on the floor beside her, and the heap of clothes on the couch. "You're going to Korea?" I asked.

Mina nodded briskly, and a rush of emotions washed over me, but mostly I felt scared; I didn't want my big sister to leave.

"Should I come, too?" I asked. "Maybe I should come, I should come, right? Because if Omma's in the hospital, then she'll be scared, you know how she hates doctors, and she'll be lonely with nobody to visit and—"

I swallowed, trying to organize my thoughts. I only realized I was trembling when Mina put her hand on my shoulder.

"I need you to stay strong, Pippa," she told me. "I don't know how long I'll be gone, and you can't afford to miss school. Besides, we simply don't have the money to buy another plane ticket to Korea right now." She took her hand off my shoulder and squeezed my hand reassuringly. She glanced over her shoulder at Jung-Hwa, who was rolling up items from the pile

166

of clothes on the couch and neatly packing them in her suitcase. "Take care of Jung-Hwa, all right? I'll be closing the laundromat temporarily while I'm gone, but there are a few regular orders that you might have to fill. I've already written them down for you, and I'll leave the keys on the counter. I trust you to handle everything while I'm away, okay?"

I lifted my chin and tried to look strong, certain that this was what I was supposed to do.

Mina gave my hand one last squeeze before bustling off to pack up her toiletries. I joined Jung-Hwa in rolling clothes and nesting them in the suitcase. Too soon, we finished and Jung-Hwa and Mina hurried out the door to go to the airport, leaving me alone. The last thing I wanted to be.

I stared blankly at one stained beige wall, wishing I had someone here to comfort me. Like Buddy or Helen. Or just someone to distract me, like Eliot.

Eliot! I suddenly remembered today was Tuesday. I grabbed my phone and checked the time. Six p.m. I'd completely missed tutoring. Unbelievable—today's events had wiped everything else from my mind.

Quickly, I punched in his phone number.

He picked up with a curt "Hello?"

"Hey, it's Pippa," I said. "I'm sorry I missed tutoring today. Something came up." I didn't tell him about my mom; I wasn't ready to tell him about her. "Can we reschedule?"

"Sure, yeah," he said, sounding distracted.

In the background, I could hear Mr. Haverford's voice—and he didn't sound happy. His yelling grew louder until I could make out every word.

"I'm not going to put up with this again. . . . No, YOU don't understand. What were you thinking? And don't tell me—"

"Is everything all right?" I asked timidly.

"Just text me a day you're free," Eliot said, ignoring my question. "I have to go."

"Oh, okay, sure," I said. "I can—"

Click.

Who was Eliot's dad yelling at? I wondered.

I sat down, wishing Eliot hadn't been so rude to me; I needed some warmth right about now. Feeling overwhelmed, I took a deep breath and tried counting to five. No use. All my problems came rushing at me, but the biggest one was Omma. What if she didn't recover from the accident? Just thinking about it was unbearable.

I didn't even realize I was crying until the tears started to drip onto my lap. With a frustrated sniff, I wiped them on the sleeve of my blazer. I couldn't afford to fall apart now. I had to stay strong, like Mina said. There was too much to do. I needed to study. Win the big game for Lakeview. And what about Throwaway? My mind drifted to the mystery texts. Hmm. Instead of waiting to see what Throwaway would do next, maybe I should try to find out who it was. But where was the time? I had to take care of Jung-Hwa for Mina. Handle the special orders for Lucky Laundromat. Repair things with Buddy. The list of tasks flitted around my mind in an endless loop.

How could I possibly do all this? How?

19

DÉJÀ VU

On Wednesday, school passed in a blur. I'd barely slept the night before, and when I checked my reflection in the bathroom mirror after lunch, I groaned at the dark circles under my eyes.

"Your mom's going to be okay, Pips," Helen tried to reassure me at lunch. I'd bought a slice of pizza, but I couldn't eat it—it just lay there on the plate, cold and leathery.

"I'm sure there are really good doctors in Seoul," Starsie added. "My dentist is Korean—he's great."

"Starsie!" Win exclaimed.

"What?" Starsie looked hurt. "I'm trying to cheer Pippa up."

"It's okay," I said with a tired smile. "I get what Starsie meant. But my mom lives in Iksan. Not Seoul."

"Is that a town?" Bianca asked. She had a funny

expression on her face, kind of squinty, like she was really trying to look concerned but didn't know how.

Mozart fluted from the cafeteria PA system, telling us lunch was over. I stood up and dumped my uneaten slice. "I can't wait for practice," I said as we walked out. "I need to blow off some steam."

"Oh, didn't you know?" Caroline asked. "Coach is out today. She always leaves a day early for Thanksgiving so she can fly to Florida and see her parents. I am so glad not to have practice for once!" She peered at me. "No offense, Pippa, but you could use a day off, too. You look terrible!"

That was Caroline—an insult hidden in every comment. I was too tired and distracted to care, though. Much.

After school I headed home, but only long enough to change out of my school uniform and grab my basketball. I know I should have used the extra time to study, but I just couldn't concentrate. Besides, Jung-Hwa had texted to say he was putting in an extra half shift at the factory. I guess he was worried about money while the laundromat was closed. Anyway, he wouldn't be home till late, and the last thing I wanted was to be alone in our claustrophobic apartment.

I dribbled down my block, past the Asian grocery. It wasn't much past four o'clock yet, but it was already starting to get dark. Hardly anyone was on the street. As I turned the corner, I thought I spotted a reflection in a store window of someone behind me, but when I glanced over my shoulder there was no one there.

I arrived at the park, half-hoping that Buddy would be at the court, but it and the toddler playground next to it were deserted. I hadn't shot hoops here in a couple of weeks, and in that time, the trees of Grey Woods had shed their leaves, leaving behind a bleak landscape of craggy branches that stretched upward like bony fingers. The November air felt raw against my cheeks. Shivering, I zipped my jacket up to my neck, stepped onto the court, and took my first shot.

Swish, swish, swish. One after another. After a few moments, I felt the fog starting to lift from my brain. *Swish, swish, swish.*

My muscles had just begun to relax when I heard something entirely peculiar.

A violin.

At first, I thought I was having some kind of weird hallucination. But the sweet, mournful music began to grow louder, drifting out of the trees. Who would be playing a violin in this nasty weather in the woods? Strange.

Clutching my basketball to my chest, I took a few cautious steps toward the sound then stopped short as I spotted a figure among the trees. I knew that sweatshirt!

Ducking behind a nearby tree trunk, I peeked out to confirm what I suspected.

Unlike when I'd met him before, his hood was down this time, and I saw that his hair was cropped into a severe buzz cut. Nevertheless, I recognized him. The violinist was my mysterious acquaintance, Green Hoodie. He was back!

Hugging the rough bark of the tree, I listened, captivated, as the beautiful melody floated toward me. It was as though the violin was telling a tragic love story, and Green Hoodie was its translator. I couldn't see his face in the gathering dark, but his body swayed slightly as the bow swept over the strings.

The piece ended on a high, soft note that slowly faded to nothing. There was a hush, and then I jumped as someone spoke. I hadn't realized Green Hoodie had company.

"Did you play that for the audition?" a male voice asked.

That voice sounded so familiar. I stopped myself from stepping closer until I could figure out who it was.

"No, I'm working on it for the next round," Green Hoodie said.

"It's good," the other voice said. My forehead crinkled. I definitely knew him. "Really good, actually."

"*Ooh!*" I clapped a hand over my mouth to stifle my squeak of surprise. Eliot! The voice was Eliot's, I was positive. But how did he know Green Hoodie?

"Thanks, but it would sound better if my fingers weren't freezing," Green Hoodie said. "I'm guessing most of the other applicants have actual indoor practice spaces." He shook his head.

Unable to resist taking a glimpse, I leaned around the trunk until I was dangerously close to being exposed. Luckily, Green Hoodie's back was to me. I could see him adjusting his bow, but Eliot was blocked from my view by a massive beech tree.

"I just wish Aunt Evelyn would change her mind," Eliot said.

"And I wish Dad would stand up to her," Green Hoodie said. His tone was bitter. "I guess we're both optimists."

My eyes widened. "Aunt Evelyn"? "Dad"?

Was Green Hoodie Eliot's *brother*?

Someone's phone dinged. "I should head home." Eliot's said. "You coming with?"

Green Hoodie shook his head. "Dad doesn't know I took the earlier bus from school. I'm not supposed to get in until eight, so I've got some time to kill. I'll hang out here and practice."

There was a clatter of shuffling feet and crunching leaves, and before I had time to scoot back behind the tree trunk, Eliot came into sight.

He stopped short when he saw me.

"Pippa?" His face darkened.

I swallowed hard. "Eliot," I replied.

Eliot looked torn between demanding to know why I was there and brushing straight past me. But before he could say anything, Green Hoodie stepped up beside him. Now that I could finally see his face clearly, I spotted the family resemblance, though Green Hoodie's hair was darker and his features were more rugged.

"Hey! Pippa Park," he said, with a surprised chuckle. "Nice to see you again."

Eliot rounded on his brother. "You know Pippa?" he demanded. Then he turned back to me with a flabbergasted expression. "You know Matthew? How?"

I opened my mouth to explain, but couldn't quite formulate the words to explain our strange first encounter.

"She helped me out a couple months ago," Green Hoodie—Matthew—said as I floundered. "We met back in September, right after I had that huge fight with Dad."

"Oh." Eliot looked only marginally less confused.

"We're friendly strangers with something major in common," Matthew added, grinning at me. "Both of us know what it's like to have our family discourage our passions."

I tried to look cool and nonchalant. Matthew made it sound as if I'd gotten him out of real trouble, and not just given him a snack, but I wasn't going to correct him—not now while Eliot regarded me with new interest. Apparently, his big brother's approval meant something major.

"Now, how do you know Pippa Park?" Matthew asked Eliot. I liked how he tacked on my last name, as if my first would be incomplete without it. It made me sound important.

Eliot's eyebrows briefly furrowed. "I tutor her in math. Plus, she's a friend from school."

I looked at him in surprise. A friend? Did Eliot consider me a friend? I hadn't known I rated even that high in his thoughts. But before I could decide how I felt about that, Eliot's text notification dinged. He reached into his pocket, stared at the screen, and grimaced.

"Dad's stressing. I really need to go. See you later," he told Matthew. He gave me a quick glance and left.

"Bye," I said, still trying to process this possible shift in our relationship.

I watched him leave before turning back to Matthew.

"How did I not know Eliot had a brother?" I asked. "I'm at your house for tutoring every Tuesday. How come I never see you?"

"I go to boarding school," Matthew replied. He frowned and touched his short hair. "Military school, in fact. I'm not home much."

"And when you do come home, you . . ." I searched around my brain, trying to find a polite way to put this. "Spend most of your time lurking in the Grey Woods?"

"I'm not lurking!" Matthew protested, wrinkling his nose in the exact same way Eliot did when he didn't approve of a question. "I'm just not *officially* home yet." He cleared his throat. "I left for Thanksgiving break a little early. Without getting permission. I had a thing in Boston."

"Your audition?" I asked.

"Oh, you heard me talking about that?" Matthew raised an eyebrow, probably wondering how long I had been spying on them.

I blushed. "Sort of." Quickly, I added, "But that still doesn't explain why you're out here in the cold, playing the violin. You have to admit, that's kind of unusual."

His grin faltered a little. "It's complicated. Sadly, this is the only place I can practice."

"Seriously?" I stared. I couldn't tell if he was joking. "I've been to your house, remember? It seems big enough to fit one person with a violin. Maybe even two."

"Ha." Matthew tried to smile, but it looked more like a grimace.

I continued to stare at him. He sighed and went on, "You're going to be sorry you asked." He carefully tucked his violin into its black case, covered it with a cloth, and closed the lid. Then he headed for the playground. "Let's sit over there and talk." He pointed to the swings.

I followed him and we sat side by side. Matthew's long legs dragged on the ground as he swung idly back and forth.

"How much do you know about the Haverford family?" he asked me.

I raised my eyebrows. Not what I was expecting. "Not a whole lot. I did hear that one story about the terrible car crash, but that's about it."

"Well, that's where the story starts," Matthew said. With one arm, he cradled his violin case against his chest.

"My grandparents—my father's mom and dad—were killed in that accident," he started to explain. "My dad was only two when it happened. My great-aunt Evelyn felt incredibly guilty. She thought it was her fault they'd been killed."

I thought about what Mrs. Lee had told me. "Why? Because they were on their way to see her concert when it happened? That seems harsh. But I guess I understand."

Matthew nodded. "From what I've been told, Aunt Evelyn's dad—my great-grandfather—put a lot of pressure on her to give up her dream of being a concert pianist. He thought it was wrong for a Haverford, especially a girl, to be out in public like that. He kept telling her that her duty was to marry a suitable man and be a good society wife."

"That's pretty medieval."

"Right?" he agreed. "It was a long time ago, but still . . . Anyhow, the accident happened, and then my great-grandfather died about a week later. Aunt Evelyn, well, she broke down. She doesn't talk about it—in fact, I only know about it from stuff I overheard my mom and dad talking about, back before they got divorced—but I'm pretty sure she was in a psychiatric hospital for a couple of years. During that time my dad was in an orphanage."

"An *orphanage*?" I repeated. Growing up in a smallish town like Victoria, it was easy to forget that those things existed.

"I know. Wild story, right? Just wait. It gets more intense," Matthew said. Standing up from the swing, he set his violin case down on the grass and started pacing restlessly back and forth.

"At some point, Aunt Evelyn got out of the hospital and moved back into the house on Satis Street. She shut herself off from most of society. She adopted my father when he was five, and she raised him. But the thing is, even though there's nothing *officially* wrong with her, you can tell she never really got past the accident."

I thought of the strange old woman, with her sequined gown and her imperious face. Yep, I had to agree. I didn't say that out loud, though.

"She's the reason my dad is so tightly wound," Matthew said. "I guess, because of her guilt, she totally bought into the whole idea about the Haverford family and its 'special obligations.'" He made air quotes with his fingers. "And she made Dad believe it, too. Brainwashed him. Maybe you noticed that he puts a lot of pressure on Eliot to be perfect. Grades, sports, everything."

I nodded. "I noticed."

"Eliot's better about dealing with it than I was," Matthew said. "He keeps his head down. I kind of rebelled. So. . . " He spread his arms wide and gave a rueful laugh. "Off to military school with me!"

I scuffed my basketball shoes against the worn patch of dirt under my swing, thinking. A lot of things I hadn't understood about Eliot were becoming clear to me now. His family life was a thousand times more messed up than mine. It didn't excuse his rudeness, but I did feel sorry for him.

Although there was something Matthew still hadn't explained. "I still don't get why you play the violin in the woods," I said.

Matthew laughed. "That's my rebellion! Aunt Evelyn is dead set against me being a musician. Against music of any kind, actually," he told me. "Have you seen the piano that's covered up in the house? And the pictures? Anything that has anything to do with music—she can't look at. But she still leaves them there. It's like she's punishing herself. I guess it's all part of her trauma."

"Oh!" I exclaimed, remembering how Eliot had reacted when I accidentally blasted Beethoven at his front door. Now I understood.

Matthew raked his hands through his hair. "And Aunt Evelyn controls all the money," he explained. "So if I'm going to get into this conservatory in Boston, I need to get a full scholarship. Which means a ton of practice wherever I can, even in the woods, if necessary, since I'm not allowed to play in the house."

"That's awful," I said. "Can you practice at your school?"

"Military school, remember? They don't give you much free time."

A sudden, irresponsible thought dashed through my mind. I almost dismissed it outright, but the look of yearning on Matthew's face mirrored mine, back when I had desperately wanted to be part of the Royals.

The more the idea bounced around in my head, the better it seemed. Well, besides the fact that if Mina ever found out, I'd be dead.

I said, "You know, I have a place you could practice. If you want."

Matthew cocked his head. I could tell that he didn't

completely believe me. Who could blame him? I was just some kid. One he barely knew.

Before I could talk myself down, I jumped off my swing and grabbed my basketball.

"Follow me," I said.

20

DEBTS

The closer we got to Lucky Laundromat, the less confident I felt about my idea. At Lakeview, I'd invested so much effort into hiding the details of my life. Now I was about to take Matthew into the laundromat. *Eliot's brother.* The place was small and dingy—they probably had a nicer laundry room at the Haverford mansion. What if he and Eliot laughed about it later?

I wanted to believe they wouldn't be that way. In any case, it was too late to turn back. Grabbing the keys from my backpack, I unlocked the doors to the laundromat and ushered Matthew inside. As I flicked on the lights, I watched carefully to see if he was disgusted by the peeling paint on the walls or the worn tile floor.

Instead, he said, "You have free run of this place? That's *cool.*"

Stepping over to one of the work tables, he set down his violin case and unclasped it.

"I want to check out the acoustics," he said, lifting out the instrument with reverence. "I think it's going to sound pretty good in here. Do you mind?"

I shook my head and hopped up on one of the dryers, eager for a second show—and this time, I wouldn't be crouching behind a tree trunk in the cold.

Resting the violin against his left collarbone, Matthew closed his eyes, and I could tell that he was getting into the right headspace. When they fluttered open again, he seemed in another world. I wondered if that was how I looked on the basketball court.

As the shimmering notes of a mournful song filled the space, I thought about the differences between the two brothers. Eliot was cool, distant, and reserved while Matthew seemed so warm and friendly. But was I wrong about Eliot? Today, I had seen a hint of warmth in him, too. Maybe Matthew brought out the softer side of his brother.

Too soon, Matthew lowered his bow and looked at me as if he'd just thought of a big problem.

"What are the hours here? Obviously, I can only play when it's closed, but I'm not sure I'll be able to get away from my house late at night."

"Not a problem," I said, glad to be able to reassure him

so easily. "This is my sister's business. It's closed while she's away in Korea. And she's not coming back for a while."

"Wow," he said. "I have to admit, this would be amazing. But are you really fine with me practicing here? Your sister, too?"

"Of course," I said, though I knew that Mina would ground me from now until retirement age if she found out that I had invited a stranger to make himself at home in the laundromat.

But he wasn't a stranger, I reminded myself. He was Eliot's brother. "Here, I'll give you my number—just text me whenever you need a space to play," I said.

"Are you sure? It's a lot to ask of you to let me in and out. It's an incredibly generous offer, but—"

"It's no problem," I said firmly. "In fact, I can make a copy of the key for you. That way you can come whenever you like."

"You're kidding me!"

Okay, now Mina wouldn't just ground me—she'd strangle me. But Matthew's excitement was contagious. I wanted to help him.

Matthew passed his phone to me. As I punched in my contact info, he shook his head a little, grinning like he couldn't quite believe his luck.

I handed it back to him and we smiled at each

other. There was a moment of slightly awkward silence. Then he said, "So—are things going okay at Lakeview?"

"What? Oh, yeah," I said. "I'm on the basketball team there."

Matthew looked pleased, but not surprised.

"I figured," he said. "Ahmad is obsessed with beating Victoria Middle."

"Completely," I agreed. "Wait. How do you know Coach Ahmad?"

"She used to be the assistant coach for the boys' basketball team back when I was in eighth grade," he told me. "She's amazing. That's why she got promoted. I don't know who wants an unbeatable girls' team more, her or Dad." He gave a crooked half-smile. "And that's why I told Ahmad about you."

I shook my head, not quite sure he was being serious, and not sure I was hearing right. "Sorry, but—are you telling me *you're* the one who got me into Lakeview?"

His smile broadened. "Ahmad needed a great player—and you needed a fresh start and a new team. When I saw you playing in the park that day, I could tell you had talent. And after you were so nice to me, I wanted to do something nice for you, too."

"But—a *scholarship*," I sputtered. "I only gave you a snack!"

"It was the right snack at the right time," Matthew said. "I had just had this huge fight with my dad, and I was kinda wallowing in self-pity, and then you shoved that neon-colored cake at me and it just . . ." He trailed off with a shrug. "Anyway, I told Ahmad about you, she talked to Dad—and the rest is history."

I was glad that I was still sitting on top of the dryer, because all of a sudden I felt a little woozy. *Matthew* had been the one to get me into Lakeview? This whole time, I believed Eliot was behind it.

How could I have gotten that so wrong?

While I was processing this, Matthew checked his phone. "I'd better run," he said. "My family thinks I'm arriving at the bus station right . . . about . . . *now*, so I've got to get to my house before they send the police dogs after me. Thanks again, Pippa Park! I'll text you!"

And he dashed out the door, leaving me staring after him.

. . .

The next day was American Thanksgiving. My family had never made a big deal of it, since we always had such a major celebration for Chuseok, but usually I went over to Buddy's at some point after his family finished their meal. We'd hang out and watch movies and play video games and stuff our faces with all the leftover pie.

Not this year. This year, Buddy wasn't talking to me. I needed to find a way to apologize to him, but with everything else that was going on in my life I just couldn't face any extra drama.

Mina had called that morning to give us an update on Omma's condition. Jung-Hwa put her on speaker phone so we could both hear.

"It was a pretty bad accident," my sister said. "She has three broken ribs, a broken arm, a cracked pelvis, and a lot of bruising, but the thing they were really worried about was a brain bleed."

"A brain bleed!" Jung-Hwa repeated, glancing at me. My heart started to pound. I chewed on my lip, trying not to freak out.

"They think they've stopped it," Mina reported, and I breathed out a huge sigh of relief. "But they were keeping her in an induced coma while they treated and monitored it."

"Can she talk?" I asked. "Can I say hi to her?"

"Not yet," Mina said. "She's out of the coma, but she's still sleeping most of the time."

"How are you doing, yeobo?" Jung-Hwa asked her. "Are you holding up okay?"

Mina sighed. "It's been a long couple of days," she replied. I could hear the tiredness in her voice. "And I think I'm going to be here for at least two more weeks. There are a lot of things I need to take care of."

"We understand," Jung-Hwa assured her. "Don't worry about Pippa and me. We're doing just fine. Right, Pippa?"

"Right," I echoed. *So far*, I thought to myself.

"Pippa, there will be a big load of dirty Thanksgiving linens coming in tomorrow morning from The Friary and Abruzzi's. I know it's a lot, but I need you to handle those orders. Laundered, pressed, tablecloths medium starch and napkins light starch," Mina instructed me. "We can't afford to lose that business."

"Got it," I said, trying not to sound dismayed. I'd helped Mina a few times with the linen orders from local restaurants. It was a ton of work. Now I would have to do it by myself.

"How's school?" Mina asked me. "Are you ready for your big math test?"

I gulped, wishing she hadn't reminded me. The test was Monday. And I'd missed my last tutoring session with Eliot . . . .

"Getting there," I said, crossing my fingers under the table. "I still have four days to study."

"Make sure you do," Mina said. "You know how important it is."

I pressed my lips together, feeling a familiar tide of

189

resentment well up. Did she really have to nag me about my grades when she was halfway around the world? I know, she was there taking care of Omma, but still . . .

Jung-Hwa picked up the phone and took it off speaker. "She's going to start right now," he said into the receiver. He smiled at me and added, "Go on, my gangaji. I'll clean up the breakfast dishes."

I headed into my room while Jung-Hwa continued his conversation with Mina. Flipping open my math book, I glanced at the practice problems Mrs. Rogers had told us to work on for the test. But I couldn't force myself to concentrate.

I pulled out my phone. **Hey, hope your family is having a good turkey day. Test Monday. Any chance you can tutor me tomorrow?** I texted Eliot.

A little while later my phone buzzed with his reply. **Busy. Can do Sunday at 2**

Sunday? Oh, well, at least it was better than nothing. I noted with a little pang that Eliot had ignored my turkey-day reference. After last night, I'd thought maybe we'd be friendlier, but it didn't seem that way.

Sighing, I turned back to my math book and tried to focus.

. . .

"Ohhhh," I groaned. I straightened up from the ironing machine, rubbing the small of my back. Now I knew what
it must feel like to be old.

It was Friday afternoon, and I'd been working at the
laundromat for more than six hours already. The napkins and
tablecloths from Abruzzi's had to be triple-washed in three
different temperatures, then starched, then dried on low,
and then pressed. Our flatbed ironing machine was old and
cranky, and you had to feed in the cloth by hand—very carefully. I'd had to redo at least five tablecloths because I fed them
in wrong and they got creased.

I spent most of my time in the back room, but every
now and then I stopped working and walked into the main
area, so I could peek out the front window. I couldn't shake the
feeling that someone was watching me.

I had barely started on the load from The Friary—
which was twice as large!—when the doorbell buzzed. "Gah!" I
dropped a napkin then relaxed. Matthew Haverford was peering in through the glass door. When he saw me, he hefted his
violin case and waved.

"You're all covered in lint," he remarked as I unlocked
the door and let him in.

I glanced down at myself. He was right—my navy
sweatshirt was blanketed with tufts of white dryer fuzz. I
looked as if I'd been rolled in a cotton candy machine.

"Tablecloths," I muttered, flushing.

"They'll get you every time," he said with a knowing nod. He began to undo the clasps on his violin case. "Hey, thanks again for letting me play here. I hope I won't be disturbing you."

"Actually, I need to get going. I hope you don't mind if I leave you on your own," I said. Jung-Hwa was working late again today, and I had told him I would make dinner tonight. Now I was wishing I hadn't, because I could use the extra study time, but I knew we didn't have the money to order takeout. After all, that was why Jung-Hwa was working so much.

"Okay, no problem!" Matthew's voice brought me back from my thoughts.

I forced a smile. "Just make sure you lock up when you leave." I held out the extra key I'd had made that morning at the hardware store, pushing away a stray image of Mina glaring at me with fire shooting from her eyes.

Outside, it was another grey, blustery day. It wasn't quite dark yet, but the streetlights had already come on. I glanced up at the sky, wondering if it was going to snow. It felt cold enough.

As the door closed behind me, something shiny on the sidewalk caught my eye. I knelt and picked it up. It turned out to be a tiny silver rectangle, engraved to look like a Queen of Clubs playing card, with a small hole drilled into the top. A lost earring?

I gazed around to see if anyone walking by might have dropped it. Mounds of black trash bags lined the curbs, but except for someone who was just rounding the corner, I didn't see anyone. Even though the street was deserted, I suddenly felt a major case of the creeps. Shivering, I tucked the little silver piece into my coat pocket and hurried back to my apartment.

21

PIPPA PARK'S GREAT GRAB

"Owwww!" I cried out.

I had forgotten that my hands were covered in gochujang and had brushed some hair out of my right eye. The fiery chili paste made me feel as though a thousand bees had stung my eyeball. "Ow, ow, ow, ow!"

Moving as fast as I could, I scrubbed my hands under the kitchen tap and then splashed cold water on my face. "Ohhhh," I moaned. It burned! Could a person go blind from chili paste?

At the sound of loud sizzling, I whipped around to the stove where I saw through my streaming, burning eyes, orangey froth bubbling out of the soup pot. "No!" I yelped, and snatched at the pot lid.

Bad move. It was *hot!* I dropped the lid on the kitchen floor with a clang and shook my fingers frantically. Steam billowed from the uncovered pot. Outside the kitchen window something flashed. Lightning? Stormy weather was in the forecast. I guess it had arrived.

I managed to turn the burner off under the pot before the kimchi-jjigae boiled out all over the stove. Cautiously, I peered into the pot. Uneven chunks of bright pink Spam—we were fresh out of pork belly—floated in a greasy liquid along with kimchi, lumps of leathery dried mushrooms, and some bits of onion. I regarded it with doubt. When Jung-Hwa made this dish, the broth was thick and savory, with crunchy golden nubbins of pork, tender vegetables, and slabs of tofu that melted in your mouth. The tofu I'd put in seemed to have crumbled into nothing, and the broth was neon orange and weirdly watery.

I heard a key turning in the lock and a moment later Jung-Hwa walked in. "What smells so good?" he called, smiling broadly at me.

I gave him a mournful look. "I tried to make kimchi-jjigae. I might have messed it up a little."

"Oh, I'm sure it will be delicious. It isn't possible to mess up kimchi-jjigae," Jung-Hwa assured me. "I'm starving! Can we eat now?"

I ladled the orange glop into two bowls and set them on the table. Jung-Hwa picked up his spoon with a flourish, scooped up a big bite, and put it in his mouth. "Mmmm!" His eyes twinkled at me as he chewed.

Then his eyes widened. No, they *bulged*. I watched in

alarm as his face turned bright red. Sweat popped out on his nose.

"What's wrong?" I asked anxiously.

Jung-Hwa swallowed then held up one finger as he went into a coughing fit.

I jumped up, filled a glass from the tap, and handed it to him. He gulped it down and pounded his chest with a fist. "Uh, how many peppers did you put in there, my gangaji?"

"Um. A handful?" I frowned. "I thought you liked it spicy."

Jung-Hwa said, "You're right, I do. I was just . . . surprised." He smiled and sipped more water. "It's good!"

I dipped a spoon in my own bowl and took a tiny, careful sip. Pain exploded in my mouth. "Ack!" I yelped, dropping the spoon. "It's *terrible*, Jung-Hwa!"

"Oh, no, don't say that," he protested. "It was a good try. You just need a little cooking practice. I watch *Chopped*. We can fix this."

He stood and headed for the pot on the stove. But even Jung-Hwa couldn't turn my kitchen disaster into a win. We ended up throwing the horrible stew away, and Jung-Hwa fried up some leftover rice with ginger and green onions and put an egg on top. By the time we finished eating, it was nearly ten o'clock, and the kitchen still looked as if something had exploded in it.

"This is too hard, Jung-Hwa," I grumbled. "I did laundry for seven hours today and managed to crease all the table linens, I ruined dinner, I still can't see out of my right eye, there's a mountain of dishes, and I haven't even had a chance to study for my math test! How are we going to live without Mina for two whole weeks?"

Jung-Hwa's big, honest face looked worried. "It seems long, but it'll go by quick, my gangaji," he assured me. "Listen, don't you worry about the kitchen. I'll clean up the dishes. You go study."

"That's not fair," I said, but kind of half-heartedly. I did feel exhausted. And I did need to study.

"It's totally fair. You worked hard today! Go on."

"Okay. Thanks, Jung-Hwa."

I headed toward my room, but at the door I turned and look back at him. His shoulders were slumped with weariness as he stood at the sink. And even though Jung-Hwa was about two decades older than me and twice as large, suddenly I felt like he was the one who needed protecting.

. . .

Saturday passed a lot like Friday: Work at the laundromat, try to study for the math test, fall asleep over my textbook. There were a few differences. One was that I didn't attempt to make dinner. In the morning, Jung-Hwa and I agreed that it would be okay to get a pizza just this once.

The other thing was that I got a text from Helen, inviting me to go to a movie marathon at the mall on Sunday with her and the Royals. **John Hughes fest,** she said. **16 Candles, Breakfast Club, Pretty in Pink. More popcorn than you can handle. Should be really fun.**

I bit my lip. It sounded like it. But there was no way I could go. Besides the fact that I didn't have time, I'd looked up the ticket prices online. It was $30 just for the movie tickets, not including snacks. That was $30 I didn't have. I'd only paid Helen back the $20 for my manicure a week ago.

Wish I could, I texted back. **Have to go to tutoring so I don't flunk the math test Monday.** I added a weepy-face emoji. Then, trying not to feel sorry for myself, I went back to the mound of cloth napkins I was ironing.

My phone buzzed a minute later. Helen again. **Aww, too bad,** she wrote. **U doing OK? News on yr mom?**

The honest answer would take hours to write, and I wasn't sure she really wanted to know. Besides, I was just too tired to get into it.

Getting better, I replied. **Thx.**

I set my phone down. As I did, it occurred to me that I hadn't gotten any messages from Throwaway in almost two months. Incredibly, in the chaos of the last few days, I'd almost forgotten about the anonymous messages. My heart beat a little faster.

Was it possible my mystery correspondent had lost interest? Had it all been nothing more than a mean bluff? *Please, please, let that be the case*, I thought. If only I could have one less thing to worry about, I might just make it through the semester . . . .

. . .

Sunday, I worked at the laundry for two hours. Finally, the linens were finished. And sure, by now the sight of a fancy tablecloth made me whimper, but I was *done*. I celebrated by watching a few episodes of *Boys Over Flowers*, even though I knew I should be studying. Or cleaning the bathroom, which was starting to look pretty seedy.

I gobbled a slice of cold pizza for lunch then got ready for my tutoring session with Eliot. I gnawed on a fingernail as I looked through my drawers. Ironically, although I'd spent my last three days at a laundromat, I didn't seem to have much in the way of clean clothes. I let out an exasperated sigh, pulled on my one pair of jeans without holes and a pink long-sleeved T-shirt with a rumpled, felt flower on the front. Then I grabbed my jacket and hurried out.

Of course, halfway to the Haverfords' house, the

bad weather that had been threatening to roll through town for days arrived with a jarring clap of thunder. By the time I turned down Satis Street, cold rain pelted down. I held my coat over my head as I sprinted toward Eliot's house. Dodging the puddles in his front yard, I ran for the door, rapping the lion's head knocker as the wind sent sheets of rain sideways.

The door opened almost immediately. Eliot was even more stone-faced than usual, and I noticed he had dark circles under his eyes. "Hey," he said in a flat voice.

No "Oh, wow, you're soaked" or "Let me get you a towel." I bit my tongue. I was coming to the conclusion that Eliot was just kind of . . . odd. He didn't bother with the usual teenage norms. Still, given what I'd learned from Matthew about the Haverford family, maybe that wasn't so surprising.

I followed Eliot through the gloomy living room and down the hall to our usual spot. As we passed Mr. Haverford's office, I heard raised voices clearly, despite the closed door. Without thinking, I slowed my steps to listen.

". . . how many school rules you've broken?" Mr. Haverford was demanding. "Absent without leave, failure to follow orders, truancy—"

"What are you gonna do about it?" Matthew's voice cut him off. "Wadsworth Academy is one step up from prison, Dad. Don't be surprised when I try to escape."

"Oh, don't be so dramatic," Mr. Haverford snapped.

"Pippa!"

I flinched then hurried around the corner to catch up with Eliot, who was waiting for me at the dining room table.

"I guess your dad found out about Matthew leaving early, huh?" I said in a low voice.

He nodded, lips tight.

"Does he know about the audition?" I pressed.

Eliot's eyes widened. "Don't even—"

"Audition?" someone said behind me.

I spun around. To my horror, Miss Haverford was standing in the far doorway. Today she wore a severe gray suit that looked as if it had been made back in the 1950s, with a be-low-the-knee-length skirt, a stiff, boxy jacket that belted at the waist, and matching gray leather pumps. As always, her hair was piled on top of her head like a strange white mushroom.

"What audition?" she demanded.

"Uh . . ." My mouth opened and closed. How much had she heard?

"Auditions for the Lakeview school play," Eliot said in a weird, strangled voice. "That's what we were talking about."

"Right," I gabbled. "It's, uh, *The Little Mermaid.*" I winced. *The Little Mermaid?* Was that even a play? "I was just telling Eliot . . . um, I'm going to try out for Ariel."

Miss Haverford's eyes narrowed. She gazed at me for a long, appraising minute. Then— "Mmmmph," she sniffed.

"How . . . progressive." Turning, she disappeared toward the back of the house, her heels clacking on the hardwood floor.

I exhaled slowly. "Think she bought it?" I whispered to Eliot.

"Just keep quiet," he whispered back.

"Sorry." I sat down and pulled out my textbook.

We'd been working—or trying to work, though it was hard to focus with the argument still audible in Mr. Haverford's study—for about ten minutes when I heard the clack of Miss Haverford's shoes coming down the hall again.

"—and then if you cross x over—" Eliot was saying, as Miss Haverford swept in. Eliot looked up and stiffened.

I followed his gaze—and dropped my pencil.

Miss Haverford was clutching Matthew's violin case.

She stalked past us toward the study. "Samuel!" she trumpeted.

I heard the study door open and a moment later Mr. Haverford appeared in the dining room doorway. "What is it, Aunt Evelyn?" he asked in a harassed tone.

"I'm glad you asked!" she snapped. Holding up the case, she brandished it, as if it were a stash of stolen goods. "I found this hidden behind a curtain. What is it, indeed?"

Eliot and I sat there, frozen in horror. I could feel my mouth hanging open.

"I have no idea," Mr. Haverford retorted, giving the case a cursory glance. Then his gaze returned to it, and his face went a little pale. "A violin case?"

Matthew stepped into the room. When he saw the case in Miss Haverford's hand, a dogged look came into his eyes. "It's mine."

"In my own house," Miss Haverford said in a low, awful voice. "Under my own roof."

"Aunt Evelyn," Mr. Haverford began, but she thrust out her hand dramatically, cutting him off.

"No, Samuel. No excuses. Clearly, your son has no respect for me or for my wishes. I don't blame him, though. This is your failure as a parent."

"Aunt Ev—" he tried again, but Miss Haverford cut him off.

"I gather that you have been to some sort of musical audition," Miss Haverford said to Matthew. "I expect you have thoughts of attending a conservatory instead of going to college."

Matthew's jaw dropped and he gave me a look of betrayal. I stared imploringly back at him. "It was an accident!" I said.

I had been trying to make myself as inconspicuous as possible, and I guess it must have worked, because Mr.

Haverford seemed to notice my presence for the first time. "Pippa!" His neck turned red. "Aunt Evelyn, this is hardly appropriate for—"

"Know this," Miss Haverford said icily. Mr. Haverford fell silent, looking trapped. "I will not allow any member of this family to pursue such a ridiculous fantasy."

Matthew stepped forward, his jaw flexing. Although I usually thought of Matthew as warm and genial, now I realized how intimidating he could be. A Haverford through and through. "Oh, really?" he said. "Do you think you can stop me?"

As if in answer, Aunt Evelyn held the violin case out to Mr. Haverford. "Dispose of this," she commanded. He obediently took it from her.

He disappeared down the hall, muttering to Matthew something that sounded like, "What were you thinking?" A moment later he returned.

"I can and I will stop you," Miss Haverford was saying to Matthew. The two of them were standing practically toe to toe, glaring at each other. Although Matthew had a good three inches on Miss Haverford, it seemed an even match. "You won't get a penny of tuition from me for *music school*." She practically spat the last two words.

"Keep your money!" Matthew flung back. "I'm going to get a scholarship. I don't need your help!"

Miss Haverford's lip curled. "We'll see about that!

Don't underestimate the reach of my influence. I can make that scholarship vanish in an instant."

The blood drained from Matthew's face, but he looked more enraged than scared.

"Pippa." I looked up to see Mr. Haverford beckoning to me. "You need to go home."

I scrambled to put my books away. Part of me wanted nothing more than to scurry away and leave the Haverfords to their chaotic family drama.

But part of me wanted—no, needed—to speak up for Matthew.

I stood and cleared my throat. "He's really good, you know," I said. I had meant to say it loud and proud, but I could barely get out a soft whisper. "I just wanted you to know."

Miss Haverford stared at me as if I had suddenly sprouted tentacles.

"Thank you for your input," Mr. Haverford said after a moment. "But this is a family matter."

I took one last look at the four of them—tall, gaunt Miss Haverford, with her poofy white hair and her cold blue eyes; Matthew, his face pale and determined; Mr. Haverford, doing his best to look as if he were in charge when it was clear he wasn't; and Eliot, sitting at the table like a statue, staring down at his hands.

Bowing my head, I left the room.

I walked through the hall, past the door to Mr. Haverford's study. It stood open, and I glimpsed Matthew's violin case on the desk. Behind me, Miss Haverford's sharp voice started up again, her high-pitched hysteria mimicking the wails of a police siren. Poor Matthew. It wasn't right for him to suffer because of something that happened to his great-aunt decades before he was even born. It wasn't fair.

I had almost reached the front door when I stopped in my tracks.

Don't do anything stupid, Pippa. This isn't your battle. Just go home, I thought, but instead, I turned and crept softly back toward the dining room.

Outside Mr. Haverford's study, I hesitated for just one more moment.

Nobody noticed me go in.

And nobody noticed me slip back out—with the violin case clutched tightly in my hand.

22

PIPPA PARK IS A PERP

Outside, the downpour had stopped. Adrenaline coursed through me and I ran, the case banging against my leg.

After a few blocks, I slowed to a walk, but as I got closer to home, the weight of what I'd just done began to sink in. What if Aunt Evelyn and Mr. Haverford figured out I'd taken the instrument? I clasped the case tightly against my chest, my breath hitching. *What if?* Of course they'd figure it out. Who else could have done it?

Would I be arrested? Would they send me to Juvie? I gulped. Math grades would be the least of my concerns there.

Maybe I should go back. Try to sneak in and return the violin to Mr. Haverford's study. But how could I get into the house? Maybe if I called Eliot, or Matthew . . .

Stopping in the middle of the street, I pulled out my phone and texted Matthew: ***I have ur violin.***

I waited, but he didn't answer. My forehead creased. What if he thought my text was some kind of ransom note? He already thought I'd betrayed him by telling his great-aunt about his audition. Maybe he thought I was some kind of budding criminal, holding him up for money?

Come get it whenever, I added. **Or I can bring it to you. Whatever works**.

I stared at the screen, willing him to write back. After a minute of nothing, I stuffed my phone back in my pocket and resumed walking. Reaching my apartment, I ran upstairs and put the violin in my room, under my bed. Then I sat down and tried to think.

My phone buzzed and I snatched it. Matthew.

You're insane . . . but awesome! Can you leave it in the laundromat? I'll pick it up on my way to the bus stop.

OK. Did they notice it's gone? I wrote back.

Nope. Dad stormed out of the house. I'll leave before he gets back. Don't worry, if they blame anyone, it'll be me. Owe you again, Pippa Park.

The breath whooshed out of me in a giant sigh of relief. Not that I wanted Matthew to get in even more trouble with his family—but at least Mr. Haverford was less likely to arrest his own son as a thief. A *thief. Even if nobody knows it, I'm still a thief*. My pulse began to pick up again. The words pounded in my head, impossibly loud, like a police officer kicking in a door.

Just then, Jung-Hwa came in from his factory shift. "How was tutoring?" he asked.

Tutoring? I stared at him. Then my heart fell all the way down to my toes. In all the craziness, I'd forgotten the whole reason I was at the Haverford house to begin with. That was two sessions in a row I'd missed, and I was almost out of time.

I gulped. "Um . . . Jung-Hwa, do you know anything about linear equations?"

. . .

I had to wait until Jung-Hwa went to take a shower before I could sneak the violin out and stash it at the laundromat. By then it was dark and the wind was picking up. I hurried down the street, fishing out my keys as I went. The streetlamp nearest to the laundromat appeared to be broken; the glass door was shrouded in blackness. I felt my heartbeat speed up as I fumbled for my keys.

I stepped into the darkened space, hugging the violin as I groped for the light. As I flipped the switch, the room temporarily filled with a burst of bright light. I blinked and glanced up at the ceiling. Had one of the fluorescent tubes blown out?

No, they were all humming away. I peered out the

window, wondering if a car had flashed its high beams at me, but there were no vehicles anywhere nearby, as far as I could tell. I pressed my face against the cold glass, but all I saw was a destroyed cardboard box skidding forward in the wind. If anyone had been outside, they were gone.

I scanned the isolated street one last time then turned to search for a good hiding place. After a moment of consideration, I stepped into a small alcove that wasn't visible from the street and tucked the case behind dryer number five. Quickly, I texted Matthew to let him know where it was. Then I locked up and sprinted back to my apartment.

I snuck back in just as Jung-Hwa emerged from his bedroom in checkered pajamas, rubbing his hair with a towel. "Were you outside?" he asked.

"Just, um, looking for my phone," I said. I held it up. "I thought I dropped it on the stairs. But it was in my pocket the whole time. Classic. Ha! Ha!"

My chuckle sounded more like rising hysteria, and I thought Jung-Hwa would see straight through my lies, but he laughed along, seeming relieved to see me smiling. As he moved past me, he touched my nose lightly with his finger. "How about I make us some dinner, my gangaji, while you do some studying?"

My smile faded. "Okay." Not that studying would make much of a difference at this point.

Plopping down on the old, worn sofa, I cracked open my notebook and stared down at the practice sheet Mrs. Rogers had handed out last week.

Solve for v: $-2(v + 1) - 9 = 5v - 10$.

I knew I was supposed to put all the Vs together, but how did the parentheses work again? And if there was a negative number, did that mean everything turned positive when I moved it to the other side?

My stomach started to clench up as my anxiety rose. Jung-Hwa was frying Spam and ginger, which I normally loved, but suddenly the smell made me feel sick. Plus, he was humming, and the noise grated on my nerves.

Jumping up, I headed into my room. Maybe I could concentrate better there.

I moved on to another problem. I'd come back to the Vs after I warmed up with something else, I decided. Maybe a graph?

Graph the equation $y = -3x$.

I thought about it. If x was one, would that make y negative three? Negative one-third? I was pretty sure one of those answers had to be right. If Mrs. Rogers gave us a multiple-choice section, I'd have at least a 50-50 chance . . . .

Lying back on my pillows, I squeezed my eyes shut and put a hand on my forehead. *Stop panicking,* I told myself sternly. *You can do this.*

My phone buzzed and I reached for it, thinking it was probably Matthew telling me he'd picked up his violin.

But the message wasn't from Matthew. As I stared at the infamous screen name, I felt numb and cold.

Throwaway 74312. This time the message was short.

The wait is finally over.

23

WHEN IT RAINS, IT POURS ON PIPPA PARK

Select the answer that best demonstrates the associative property of addition.

I stared at the four potential answers on my test, then out the window. I had no clue which one was correct.

The day was brilliant and cold, with a blustery wind that tugged at the few remaining leaves on the maple trees that lined the walkway. I wished it could blow the fog out of my mind as well. My eyes felt dry and sandy, and a dull headache throbbed at my temples. Between anxiety about the test and fear of what Throwaway had planned for me, I hadn't gotten more than two hours of sleep last night.

"Ten minutes, everybody," Mrs. Rogers announced.

I looked down at my still-unfinished math test. Four questions remained. I started to read, but scanning the equations felt like bobbing for apples: The answers were impossible to get, too slippery to capture.

The next thing I knew, Mrs. Rogers was saying, "Pass up your tests, everyone."

What? I blinked. Had ten minutes passed already? I started to sweat. I still hadn't answered the final questions.

"Now, everyone. That includes you, Pippa."

Desperate, I scribbled in random values for x and y, crossed my fingers, and passed the paper up.

"What'd you get for the problem about the bunnies?" Helen asked as we left the classroom.

"I don't remember," I mumbled. In fact, I didn't even remember reading a problem about bunnies.

I'd done badly on the test, that much I was sure of. I didn't know how badly. But I doubted I'd gotten an 80. That was the lowest grade I needed to keep my GPA in the acceptable range.

Would they kick me out right away? Or would they give me till the end of the semester to pull my grade back up? Could I even manage that?

And what about Throwaway? **The wait is finally over.** The text had been sent last night, so when was the ball going to drop?

I let out a long sigh. One way or another, it seemed like my life here at Lakeview was going to end quickly.

Which meant I should have been frantic. But today,

for some reason, it all seemed muffled somehow, behind a grey veil. *There's nothing more I can do*, I thought. *Whatever happens, happens.*

"You okay, Pips?" Helen asked me. "You seem a little quiet."

"Just tired." As if to illustrate the point, an enormous yawn nearly cracked my jaw.

"You better start getting some sleep," she scolded me. "We need you at your best for Friday."

"Friday?" I repeated blankly.

Helen punched my shoulder lightly. "The game! The season opener! Hello?"

"Oh, right!" I forced a laugh. "Don't worry. I'll be fine."

I spent the rest of the morning struggling to stay awake in my classes. I did doze off a little in French, causing Monsieur Trouillefou to punish me by making me read a dialogue where my character was a terrible snorer. My classmates, of course, thought that was hilarious. *Moi? Pas tant.*

At last, the lunch bell rang, and I sleep-walked toward the cafeteria, feeling zombie-like. My sneakers dragged with every step, scuffing up the otherwise pristine floors. In the doorway, I nearly collided with Olive—she was leaving as I was entering. "My bad," I said, but she brushed past me without a word.

I joined a line to buy something to eat but realized that I had only one crumpled dollar bill and some loose change. Even though I'd done more laundry in the past three days than I normally did in two weeks, with Mina gone, there was no one to pay me for my work. I contented myself with an apple. Hopefully, Helen would let me steal some of her fries. She usually did.

As I was heading toward the Royals' table with my apple and a cup of water from the fountain, I spotted Eliot entering the big, high-ceilinged room.

He was with his usual posse of jocks. Usually, I wouldn't have dared to go up and talk to him when he was surrounded by his friends like that, but today I was feeling reckless. Or maybe unhinged. Either way, I didn't really care about the cool factor. Or what Bianca or Caroline thought. I just wanted to know what had happened with Matthew after I left the Haverford house—Matthew had picked up his violin from the laundromat last night, but I hadn't gotten to see him or ask any questions.

I walked by Eliot and, catching his eye, jerked my head to the side and raised my eyebrows at him. He looked at me with intense reluctance.

"Dude," his friend with the short red hair said. "Either that girl is having some kind of spasm or she wants to talk to you."

A faint flush stained Eliot's cheeks. Stepping over to me, he turned so his back was to his friends. "What's up?" he asked, sounding a little embarrassed.

"I wanted to know if Matthew's okay," I said in a low voice.

Eliot rubbed his hand over his face. His eyes were faintly bloodshot, with dark circles beneath. He looked as tired as I felt. "Depends on your definition. He went back to school last night," he said. "And he took his violin from Dad's study with him. It surprised us all, but I thought Aunt Evelyn was going to have a heart attack. People don't usually cross her."

"About that," I started to tell him the truth about the violin, but the red-haired dude began calling from the table.

"Yo, Haverford! Stop making out with your girlfriend and get over here! Jason's about to eat this habanero!"

I could feel my face growing hot, and Eliot's ears went red.

"I gotta go," he muttered. He turned away and was scowling as he took his seat. "Dude, shut up," I heard him grumble as the red-head said something else.

Biting my lip, I continued toward the Royals' table. I placed my water and apple on the table and pulled out my chair. It wasn't until I sat down that I noticed Caroline glaring at me. Bianca's expression was frosty, and Win and Starsie were studiously looking at their food. Only Helen seemed normal.

Caroline leaned across the table. "Poor Pippa," she said with fake sweetness. "You look terrible! Are you feeling okay? Or is it just because Eliot blew you off? Again?"

Caroline glanced at Bianca and the two of them exchanged tiny, snarky smiles.

I took a bite of my apple, chewed without tasting it, and told myself to ignore them. But Caroline wouldn't let it go.

"Oops. Did I touch a nerve?" she asked. She studied my face, and when I finally met her gaze, I could tell she was really enjoying this. "I'm sorry. I don't mean to offend you, it's just, your constant groveling toward Eliot? Not a good look, Pips. Take it from a friend. Besides, why would Eliot be interested in you, when he already has someone like Bianca?"

I swallowed some apple, took a breath, and opened my mouth to politely tell Caroline that I didn't need her advice. Or, at least, that's what was supposed to come out.

I don't know if it was the lack of sleep, the stress of my math disaster, embarrassment at what Eliot's friend had said, or a combination of those things along with everything else that was going wrong in my life, but suddenly I just snapped.

"You know what? You have no idea what I said to Eliot, or what he said to me, so back off. And stop calling me your friend when all you want is drama. Because I am so *sick* of you making me feel stupid, and I have enough problems without adding you, Bianca's attack dog, to the list." To my horror, I felt tears pricking the corners of my eyes. The last thing I wanted to do was break down here, in the cafeteria, with everyone watching. "I'm out." I sprung to my feet and left.

I stalked through the front hall, pushed open the doors, and stepped onto the wide veranda of the school, breathing in the frosty air. What had I just done?

Well, for one thing, I'd just tanked any chance I had at staying in with the Royals. Since I was almost certainly going to be kicked out of Lakeview soon, it probably didn't matter. But I would really miss my friendship with Helen, and even Win and Starsie.

I stayed outside in the cold for the rest of the lunch period, just gazing out over the grounds and trying not to think about anything. Eventually, the strains of Mozart told me I had to go back in and try to act normal.

As I walked up the stairs to my English class on the second floor, I noticed kids in the hall doing double-takes and staring at me. Bianca and Caroline didn't waste any time dissing me, I guessed. I knew I should be feeling bad about it, but I was so tired, all I could manage was mild discomfort.

I entered Mr. Douglas's class and took a seat in my usual chair. To my surprise, Divya plopped down in the spot next to me. When she saw me looking at her, she gave me a slight smile. "Hey," she said.

"Hey," I responded, baffled. Did she no longer hate me now that Bianca and Caroline did?

I waited for her to say something, but she just busied herself with pulling out her notebook. I saw a few other kids glancing at me and whispering, and my confusion turned back into resignation. The Royals really did rule the school.

Mr. Douglas hurried in and wrote "Captain Wickham" on the board, and class began.

I had better luck staying awake here. For one thing, I usually enjoyed English (except the times when I'd had to partner with Divya). For another, the fact that I'd only eaten an apple since seven o'clock that morning meant that my stomach was starting to cry out for food. I'd have to see if I could scrounge up some crackers or something before practice, I realized.

Class was almost over when a student came in and handed a note to Mr. Douglas. He read it and then glanced at me.

"Pippa, you're wanted in the headmaster's office," he said.

"Me?" I said stupidly. My scalp prickled. What could Mr. Haverford want with me?

I flashed back to the last time I'd been summoned out of class. Had something else happened with Omma? With Mina or Jung-Hwa? I felt a wash of dread.

Gathering up my books, I hurried down the stairs, toward the lobby. Ms. Elkington smiled at me as I approached her desk. Was it my imagination, or did she look sympathetic?

When she said, "Go on in, he's waiting for you," my stomach heaved with anxiety. Suddenly I was glad I hadn't eaten much for lunch.

I stepped into the headmaster's office. My eyes darted from the college and graduate school diplomas hanging on the wall to the granite pen set on his desk.

Mr. Haverford sat in a massive black chair, his back rigid, with both hands palms down on the desk. "I'm not going to keep you long, Miss Park," he said, before I had even sat on the hard wooden chair in front of him.

Alarm bells of a different kind went off in my head. This was the first time he had called me "Miss Park." Usually he called me Pippa.

"Is this about my math grade?" I asked, my voice quavering a little. Surely, Mrs. Rogers hadn't graded our tests already? Maybe she had just done mine, knowing that I was going to fail.

He sighed. "No, Miss Park, it's not about your math grade."

He flipped over a piece of paper on his desk and turned it around to face me. It was a printout that looked like a newspaper, with headlines and photos and columns of type.

Or rather, one headline that screamed across the page:

JUST WHO IS PIPPA PARK???

I stared at it for a moment without comprehension. Was there some celebrity with the same name as me?

Then my gaze focused on the first picture. Of me. In the kitchen of my apartment, sweatshirt covered in lint and eyes swollen, gochujang steam billowing from a pot on the stove, the lid frozen in mid-air as I dropped it. Behind me you could see the cracked linoleum floor and the ancient, chipped porcelain sink.

"Well?" Mr. Haverford said. "Can you explain this?"

I looked up at him, bewildered. "Someone must be following me," I said, confused. "I don't know who, though, if that's what you're asking. . . ."

Mr. Haverford shook his head. "I mean *this*." He tapped the second photo, toward the bottom of the page.

Obediently, I lowered my gaze again. Mr. Haverford was pointing to an overexposed flash photo of me in the laundromat, clutching the black violin case to my chest, keys dangling from my hand, my hair flying every which way. My eyes glowed in the flash like those of a wild animal. The caption read: *Rare spotting at the Lucky Laundromat. Is this the real Pippa Park?!*

Now I knew why Mr. Haverford was so upset.

Matthew's violin.

I tried to swallow, but my mouth was dry, and a lump had already begun to form in my throat.

"Recognize that case?" Mr. Haverford pressed. "You took it from my study, didn't you?"

"I—I—" I stammered.

"This is serious, Miss Park. Very serious. You stole something from my home. It's called theft—and it's criminal."

"But Matthew—" I began.

"Yes, I assumed my son had taken it at first, but he didn't, did he? The photograph tells the real story. I must say, this behavior goes beyond youthful hijinks. It's deeply troubling, Pippa. Do you have any explanation for what you did?"

I stared down at my hands, blinking back tears.

I hadn't meant to commit a crime. I just wanted to help Matthew.

"Well?" Mr. Haverford asked.

My lips trembled, but I couldn't force my mouth open. Weird waves of goosebumps ran from my scalp down over my arms, and it felt as if a huge lump had formed in my throat. So I just shook my head silently.

Mr. Haverford exhaled through his nose. "I don't take any pleasure in this, Pippa. But I'm going to have to suspend you from school while the disciplinary committee and I decide what to do about you."

He stood up and opened his door. "Ms. Elkington has notified your guardian, Mr. Kim. He'll be here to pick you up shortly. You can wait for him by the reception desk."

I stood up and moved stiffly out of his office. In the lobby, the walls seemed to be pushing together, boxing me in on all sides. I tried to breathe, but every time my lungs expanded, my ribs ached.

Throwaway had made good on their threat, that was for sure. I wondered where they had posted their "newspaper." Had everyone at school seen it? How had it ended up on Mr. Haverford's desk? Eventually, I'd find out the answers, I knew. But right now, I just wanted to go home and hide.

Hoping Jung-Hwa would already be waiting for me, I looked toward the reception desk, but he wasn't there, and neither was Ms. Elkington. However, a familiar figure was sorting through notices on the bulletin board, taking down old items and posting new ones.

"Pippa," Olive Giordano said. "You look upset. Is something wrong?"

Her voice had a strange, eager tone. And her eyes, as she peered at me, were bright with excitement. As she reached up to remove an old notice, I zoomed in on the bracelet circling her wrist. The silvery charms tinkled against each other. I had a sudden image of myself, stooping to pick up a tiny, silver playing card from the street outside the laundromat. I had thought it was an earring. Now I knew the truth.

I shivered, remembering those times I had felt someone was following me. Watching me.

"It was you," I said. "You're the one who took those pictures."

"Me?" Olive said, her eyes widening just a shade too much.

"You're Throwaway," I stated. "Aren't you?"

24

PIPPA PARK IS DOWN AND OUT

"Throwaway? I don't know what you're talking about," Olive retorted. But she couldn't stop a smirk from creeping across her face.

"You stalked me," I said. "You sent me horrible messages. You took pictures of me! Why, Olive? Why would you do all that?"

"Why?" Olive echoed, abandoning her act. "After what you did to me? Pretending to be my friend just until you got in with the Royals, and then dropping me?"

"I didn't—" I started to say. But then I stopped. Actually, I had pretended. I never really liked Olive all that much; I had just kind of let her commandeer me, back when I didn't know anyone else.

But, I realized, she'd pretended, too, in her own way. She had never seemed interested in *me* as a person. She'd seen me as a tool to make herself more popular and score a seat at the Royals' lunch table.

"Well, I guess we're even," I said, speaking as much to myself as to her. "Actually, I guess you win. Since I've been suspended, maybe even expelled."

Olive blinked. Her mouth fell open, and she stared at me with widened eyes that looked genuinely surprised. "But—"

Before she could finish, Ms. Elkington came hurrying down the hall.

"Olive, you need to get to class," she said reproachfully. "I've told you before, you can't use your student ambassador duties as an excuse to skip English." Moving behind her desk, she made a shooing motion with her hands. "Go on now."

Closing her mouth, Olive picked up her book bag and started for her classroom. After a few steps she turned and looked over her shoulder at me. Her expression was puzzled. Then she left, and I was alone, waiting for Jung-Hwa to pick me up and take me away from Lakeview. Maybe for the last time . . . .

While I waited, I started scrolling through my phone, more to look like I was doing something rather than out of any real interest. Within seconds, though, I found out why everyone had been staring at me and whispering all day.

A link to the article Mr. Haverford had shown me, *Just Who Is Pippa Park?* was posted as a comment on the school blog. And shared all over social media, of course. The time stamp indicated that it had been up for a couple of hours, which meant it had been posted during lunch.

I remembered Olive shoving past me as she left the cafeteria earlier that day. She must have been heading off to put it up at that very moment. *That's right,* I thought. *Olive told me she used to publish a school newsletter.* She'd had all the tools she needed to take me down.

I began to read.

Just who is Pippa Park? She says she's from Boston. But guess what—she grew up right here in Victoria. (This was followed by the picture of my cooking disaster.)

She says her sister runs her own business. You know what kind of business? A laundromat! That's right, the fabulous Pippa Park spends her free time folding other people's underwear.

This paragraph was followed by the photo of me with the violin in the laundromat. The picture that had gotten me suspended. I sucked in a breath as I realized that Olive didn't have any idea about the true consequences of that photo. She knew nothing about me stealing the violin from Mr. Haverford's study. To her it was just an unflattering picture of me in an embarrassing location. No wonder she had looked so surprised when I told her I was suspended.

I forced myself to finish the article.

Everyone thinks she went to a fancy school in Boston. But

the truth is, until a month ago she went to public school. And not just any public school. She went to Victoria Middle—where she was their star basketball player!

Who is Pippa Park? She's a liar, that's who, and now this liar is playing for the Lakeview Jaguars. The rumor is that she's planning to throw the game so her old school wins. It may seem hard to believe that anyone could be such a snake, but with someone as fake as Pippa Park, would you be surprised?

I'd been worried that the team would be suspicious of me if they knew I had played for Victoria Middle—and now Olive made it sound totally believable. This clinched it. I was finished at Lakeview. Even if Mr. Haverford didn't expel me, I'd be an outcast for the rest of my time here. No one would ever speak to me again.

When Jung-Hwa arrived, he took one look at my face and offered me his hand in silent sympathy. I followed him out to the car and we drove home, still in silence. My eyes registered the passing of houses, trees, streetlights, but my mind couldn't focus.

We entered the apartment, and I collapsed onto the couch, staring numbly at the wall.

Jung-Hwa moved around for a few minutes, rinsing out his soup thermos and hanging up both our coats. Then he settled down next to me and touched my shoulder gently. "My gangaji, can you tell me what happened?"

I picked at one of my cuticles. "Jung-Hwa, would you ever be so mad at me that you would stop loving me?"

Jung-Hwa didn't stop to think about his answer.

"Never," he said.

His warmth should have reassured me. Instead, it made me feel even worse. The shame I'd felt about his home-made lunches, irritation at his clumsy gestures of affection, and embarrassment at his grimy clothes—they all sent a wave of guilt over me. He was the kindest man I'd ever known. Why did any of the rest of it matter?

"Even if I really, really messed up?"

"Even then. Pippa, whatever happened, just tell me," Jung-Hwa said. "Then we'll go from there."

I licked my dry lips, trying to find the right words. Finally, I exhaled.

"Jung-Hwa," I said. "I really messed up."

"So tell me," he repeated.

And somehow, I did. Soon, words were spouting from my mouth like water from a faucet. Or, more like, water crashing through a dam—unstoppable.

At first, I only meant to tell him part of the story. Instead, I found myself revealing everything, from my impossible crush on Eliot, to how I had let my new friends at Lakeview believe I was someone I wasn't, to the way things had gone wrong with Buddy. I talked for the better part of an hour.

Jung-Hwa remained quiet the entire time, simply listening, and occasionally bobbing his head.

When I got to the part about being suspended, Jung-Hwa wiped a tear off my cheek, his expression tender.

"And Jung-Hwa, the worst part is, it really is all my fault," I said. "I got caught up in this idea that I could be someone different." My bottom lip quivered. "I kept thinking that if I just made myself into someone else, then one day I would become a Royal. I would be Eliot's girlfriend. I would belong at Lakeview. But I never will. It's not my world. And now everyone thinks I'm a terrible person."

Jung-Hwa gave my hand a brief squeeze. That made me cry even more for some reason. Shuddering, I wrapped my arms around myself. "The whole school knows I came from Victoria Middle, and they think I'm going to throw the game—not that it matters now, since I won't be playing in it. But I can't stand what they must think of me."

I slouched lower on the couch.

"And Omma," I went on. "I'm so worried about her. She's so fragile already. What if this makes her worse? I just wanted her to be proud of me. . . ."

I finally went silent. Jung-Hwa tugged at the collar of his shirt.

"That's a lot going on, my gangaji," he started tentatively. He bobbed his head again, seeming to struggle with what he wanted to say. "First, Omma is going to be fine, and she's already proud of you. So let's wipe that thought out of your head. Along with this 'terrible person' nonsense. You made some mistakes, Pippa. Everyone makes mistakes." He took a deep breath. "I'm sorry about your friends. But if they're truly your friends, then they'll listen to you, try to understand, and hopefully give you another chance. If not, you're too good for them, anyway. But I know that's not the most helpful advice."

I blinked up at him, trying to clear my eyes. "You think I'm too good for them?" I asked, my voice breaking on the word good. "When I've done everything wrong?"

Jung-Hwa reached forward to hug me, but I pushed him away, unable to bear the guilt. Fresh tears started to stream down my cheeks as I thought of all the ways I had failed him over the last two months.

"You wouldn't hug me if you knew all the terrible thoughts I've had," I told him. "I lied to you on Chuseok. The reason Buddy didn't come was because he was already mad at me. And it wasn't that my new school friends were too busy. I never invited them. I'm sorry."

Jung-Hwa's bushy brows pushed together. "Because you were ashamed of us?"

I lowered my head. "They're all rich, and I've heard them make fun of scholarship students. I thought that they would find out I work in a laundromat and think they were too good to hang out with me, and I worried if they saw our little apartment, they'd sneer." I swallowed a sob. "I was ashamed."

"Do you still feel that way?" Jung-Hwa asked.

I thought about it for a minute and was surprised by the answer. "No," I said. I thought of the Haverford family's giant house, filled with tension and ghosts and that weird, stale smell. My apartment might be shabby, but at least it smelled like good food and felt like warmth and family.

"Honestly," I said. "There's nowhere I'd rather be right now than sitting in our living room with you. This—" I gestured around me. "Is great. Everything outside of this? Not so much." I sighed. "I just wish everything would stop falling apart. I have no school to go to now. Everyone at Lakeview is gossiping about me. Buddy won't even talk to me. . . ."

Jung-Hwa's expression melted. He tapped me on the nose. "Remember, my gangaji, the lower you fall, the more room you have to rise. This will pass, eventually."

"I don't think that's true."

"Time always helps," Jung-Hwa said, decidedly. "Things always look different from farther away." Jung-Hwa paused. "That's for the things you can't change. But some things you can."

I could guess what he was referring to.

"Do you mean the stuff with Buddy?"

He nodded. "That's one thing. You should talk to him. Apologize."

I took in Jung-Hwa's words of wisdom. It's not that he gave me any shining nuggets of advice that would magically solve everything for me. In fact, most of what he said was stuff that I already knew deep down. But there was something about the way he said them that made me feel better. Stronger.

Then he added. "There's someone else you need to talk to. Someone who loves you as much as I do, even if she shows it in different ways."

My stomach did a flip.

"Mina?" I asked in a small voice.

Jung-Hwa just looked at me patiently.

"Now?" I said.

He glanced at the clock on the kitchen wall. "It's four a.m. in Korea. Maybe now isn't the best time. We'll make the call tonight. Together."

I swallowed hard. "Thank you," I said.

Jung-Hwa squeezed my shoulder gently. Then I headed into my room, took out my phone, and wrote a text to Buddy.

I'm so sorry. You were my best friend, but I blew it. I did everything I could to push you away. I was chasing after new friends, and I treated you badly.

I can do better, though, if you let me try. I'll understand if you don't want to bother. I don't know. I guess all I can say is I miss you. And I'm really, really sorry. And I hope that maybe somewhere deep inside you still miss me too.

Always your friend,

Pippa.

I read the text over. Was it too short? Too long? Did it sound fake? Would he even read it? *Just send it*, I told myself.

Taking a deep breath, I hit *Enter* before I could change my mind.

25

GAME CHANGER

"You ready to go, Pippa?" Jung-Hwa stuck his head into my room. "We don't want to be late."

It was Friday, the day of my disciplinary meeting with Mr. Haverford. I looked down at myself. I was wearing a plain red T-shirt and jeans. I'd debated wearing my Lakeview uniform, but that seemed kind of presumptuous. I was pretty sure I wouldn't be going back to school there.

I stood and headed to the door. "As ready as I'll ever be."

Jung-Hwa nodded but lingered in the doorway. His expression had turned apologetic. What now?

"I spoke to your sister this morning," he said. "And she was, well, extremely clear that she expects a call from you after the meeting."

I bit my lip, then nodded. "Noted."

The week of being at home, in limbo, had been

strange and mostly unpleasant, but surprisingly, my conversation with my sister hadn't been as awful as I had anticipated. Jung-Hwa had spoken to her first, taking the phone into his bedroom so that he could have some privacy. He was gone for a long time, leaving me biting my nails in the living room, imagining all the ways Mina would find to call me a failure. I could practically see her thumbing through a thesaurus, hunting for synonyms.

Finally, Jung-Hwa came out and passed the phone to me. My hand trembled as I put it to my ear.

"I'm sorry," I blurted, without even saying hello.

There was a pause on the other end. Then Mina said, "I'm sure you are."

"I've been really stupid," I added.

"I agree," Mina said. There was another, longer pause. Then, to my amazement, she added, "Maybe we both have been." Her voice sounded stiff, strained.

"I'll never—wait. What?"

"I said 'maybe,'" Mina quickly added. Then she sighed. "We both know you have room to improve in school. But that doesn't mean you're not trying. I put a lot of focus on the ways you can do better. Sometimes I forget to tell you about the ways you make me proud."

I pulled the phone away from my ear and stared at it for a moment. Was I in some kind of alternate universe?

"Mina, is that you?" I ventured.

That earned me a more familiar snort.

"Listen, Pippa. I'm not very good at this kind of thing, but I need you to know that I love you, and I hope you realize why I push you so hard. I just want you to have the kind of life that Omma meant for you to have. You have opportunities that she never had—that I never had—and I don't want you to waste them." Mina exhaled. "But I guess I was burdening you with my own dreams, too. And that's not fair to you."

"Wow. You're right," I said, stunned that Mina and I were actually on the same page for once. "It wasn't fair."

"But you should still try not to flunk out of middle school," Mina's voice grew steadier, "for your own benefit."

Mina had some other choice words about how "incredibly, almost astonishingly unwise" I had been to take the violin from Mr. Haverford's study—but all in all, it was the best conversation I'd ever had with my sister. When I hung up, I felt as if a heavy weight had been lifted from my shoulders.

Another thing that had made me feel a bit better was that I'd gotten a text from Helen on Tuesday. I hadn't seen it until I finally went to bed at midnight. It had said simply, **Wanna talk?**

It had been too late for a phone call, and I wasn't sure I was ready to face anyone from my team yet anyway. **Maybe later**, I'd written.

Helen's reply came immediately. It was just an emoji heart, but it let me know that, at least to Helen, I wasn't a complete villain.

That was Tuesday, though, and now it was Friday. Three long days of me sitting around my apartment, watching reruns of *Teen Titans*, trying to stop replaying what had happened. Trying, too, not to obsess over the fact that Buddy hadn't replied to my text. Not to mention stressing over this disciplinary hearing.

I followed Jung-Hwa down to the car. As he drove, he tried to make conversation, but I couldn't focus on anything but my own nerves. My nails dug into the palms of my hands, leaving crescent-shaped indents in the flesh.

As we made our way into the administrative office, I realized that Jung-Hwa looked almost as anxious as me. He had changed from his work clothes to an only-slightly-wrinkled green button-down, a pair of dark-washed jeans, and his good tennis shoes. He had paired this with a tie in an effort to look somewhat formal, but the result was more like a kid dressing up as a "grown-up" for Halloween.

Ignoring the little part of me that cared who might see, I clasped Jung-Hwa's hand and held it as we walked up to the front door. I tried to take in everything I could, from the sun slanting through the tall windows to the mellow polished wood of the display cases. This was probably the last time I would ever see the inside of Lakeview.

The airy front hall was largely deserted; my former

classmates were in the middle of last period. Ms. Elkington smiled as we walked up to her desk, and I thought about how far I'd fallen since the first time I'd been here, back when I had been at my most optimistic. I felt a wave of sadness. Despite how awful the last week had been, I still loved Lakeview. I would miss the gorgeous views, the surprisingly delicious food, Coach Ahmad's demanding practices. I'd even miss Mrs. Rogers's math class. And, of course, Helen and Eliot and . . .

I swallowed. No use torturing myself with the good memories now.

While we waited for Mr. Haverford to call us in, Jung-Hwa played with the knot on his tie—loosening and tightening it until, by the end, it was as crumpled as his shirt. I had never seen him look so nervous.

Before I could think of anything that might reassure him, Mr. Haverford's door opened, and he motioned us inside.

"Thank you for having us, sir," Jung-Hwa started awkwardly as we sat down in the hardwood chairs. His voice was more strained than usual. "We appreciate the opportunity to talk about Pippa's situation."

Mr. Haverford inclined his head and gestured for Jung-Hwa to continue.

"Well, first of all, Pippa would like to apologize for the, uh, incident at your house. So . . ."

Both Jung-Hwa and Mr. Haverford turned to me, putting me on the spot.

"Right." I bobbed my head. "Yes. Um." I exhaled. "I'm so sorry for what I did. It was completely out of line. I should never have gone into your study, much less touched something that wasn't mine. That was wrong."

Mr. Haverford's gaze softened somewhat. But like an idiot, I had to keep going.

"But I just want to say that I didn't do it for myself," I added.

"Pippa," Jung-Hwa said nervously.

But Mr. Haverford didn't seem surprised. In fact, his shoulders sagged slightly.

"Yes," he said. He cleared his throat. "About that. I spoke to my son and I think I understand what your intentions were. I know now that you were trying to return the instrument to Matthew, not trying to steal it. It was impulsive, maybe even foolish, but it was still a generous thing to do."

I exchanged a startled glance with Jung-Hwa.

Mr. Haverford leaned back in his chair and steepled his fingers in front of him.

"Pippa," he said, "I'll admit that I've been wrestling with what to do about your situation."

Wrestling? I perked up. A tiny flower of hope began to bloom in my chest. Did this mean my fate might not be decided yet?

"On the one hand, you haven't had the smoothest beginning here at Lakeview. The incident with Olive was hurtful and disgraceful, and we've already held a separate disci-plinary meeting with Miss Giordano. But at the same time, Mrs. Rogers tells me your work in her class has been, let's say, sub-optimal."

I sagged. "I failed the math test, I guess."

Mr. Haverford pursed his lips. "Actually, you got a C minus." Noticing my look of pleased surprise, he added, "which is still below the cutoff for maintaining your required GPA."

"But it's not failing," Jung-Hwa objected, then looked startled at his own boldness.

"It's not," Mr. Haverford agreed. "And, as Mrs. Rogers pointed out, there are significant extenuating circumstances. She reminded me that one of your primary guardians has been away, caring for your mother after a serious accident."

"That's right," Jung-Hwa piped up. "And Pippa's been picking up the slack both at the laundromat and at home. She even cooked dinner!"

"Yes, I saw the photo," Mr. Haverford commented dryly. I couldn't hold back a burst of laughter at that, though I turned it into a cough. Mr. Haverford could make jokes!

He hesitated, then added with a touch of embarrass-ment, "Also, Eliot reminded me that, thanks in part to a . . . disturbance . . . in my own family, you were forced to miss two tutoring sessions in a row right before your test."

I blinked at him. "Eliot talked to you about me?"

"Eliot, and others, too. You've made a strong impression in the short time you've been here," Mr. Haverford said. He held up his hand and started ticking names off on his fingers. "I've had visits, phone calls, and emails from Helen Pelroy, Winona Hussein, Bianca Davis—"

Bianca? Bianca stood up for me? Now I was starting to think I was in a parallel universe. Then I realized she probably wanted to make sure I stayed on the team. Apparently, her need for a win against Victoria Middle trumped her dislike for me.

Mr. Haverford went on reciting the names of everyone who had come to him in my defense. "—Mrs. Rogers, Coach Ahmad, and a few others I'm forgetting at the moment. Not to mention my own sons—both of them." He coughed again. "And, of course, your sister is a very . . . persuasive person."

At that, Jung-Hwa let out his own snort of laughter. "She is, isn't she?"

Mina hadn't told me she was going to call the headmaster, but I should have known she couldn't stay silent.

Mr. Haverford tugged at his tie and glanced at me. "Let me just say this. If you possess a fraction of Mrs. Kim's ability to argue, Pippa, you should consider law school in the future.

"Anyway, the long and the short of it is, I've been

persuaded to give you another chance. Mrs. Rogers has agreed that you can take a make-up test in two weeks."

"You're kidding. I mean, please don't be. But . . . really?" I looked to my right, and then to my left, searching for hidden cameras. Was this a new reality show? *Punk'd: Private School Edition.*

"That's wonderful news!" Jung-Hwa cried. His face split into a huge grin. "Thank you, sir. Thank you!"

"There is one condition, though." Mr. Haverford held up a finger.

Uh-oh. I knew this was too good to be true.

"That you play to win against Victoria Middle tonight," Mr. Haverford said.

I shook my head. "Mr. Haverford, please believe me. I would never throw a game, no matter what it said in that article."

"I never believed you would," Mr. Haverford said, looking surprised. "But Eddie Rochester was my teammate when I was on the Lakeview basketball team, and he never let anyone forget how much better he was than the rest of us." He raked a hand through his hair until it stood straight up. "I've had a running bet with him for seven years, now. I just want to see the look on his face when we finally cream him!"

Eddie Rochester. My eyes widened. He was Victoria Middle's principal!

"Oh, that reminds me. Coach Ahmad gave me something for you." Mr. Haverford reached under his desk and pulled out a plastic shopping bag, which he handed to me.

I peered in. There, neatly folded, was my game uniform.

Mr. Haverford glanced at his watch. "You have about ten minutes until warm-ups," he said. "I would get going."

26

PIPPA PARK IS BACK IN THE GAME

I didn't waste any time. I burst out of Mr. Haverford's office and sprinted down the hallway. Behind me, I could just barely hear Jung-Hwa cry, "Go get 'em, gangaji!" At the same time Mr. Haverford yelled, "No running in the halls!"

As I approached the sports center, though, I slowed to a walk, and not just because Mr. Haverford had told me to. In my excitement, I had momentarily forgotten about Olive's article. About the fact that everyone on my team now thought I was a liar—and maybe even believed I would throw the game to Victoria Middle.

I steeled myself and pushed through the glass doors. I'd just have to prove them wrong on the court. I'd play so good, no one could possibly doubt me. After that . . . well, I'd have to see what happened.

My stomach was doing flips again, so before I could lose my nerve, I burst into the locker room. My teammates turned around at the noise. Eleven pairs of eyes widened at the sight of me, and everyone went silent. For about a second. And then the locker room erupted.

"Pippa! I can't believe you made it!"

"I was rooting for you!"

"I'm so glad you're back!"

"I thought you were the one who said—"

"Shut up!"

Helen bounded up and threw her arms around me. "I had my fingers crossed the entire day!" she whispered.

I looked from one smiling face to the next, and even though I was obviously happy that everyone was cheering for me instead of chucking basketballs at me, I couldn't help but be a little confused.

It was Starsie who cleared things up. "Coach explained *everything*," she chirped. "About how she recruited you from Victoria Middle and told you to keep quiet about where you came from."

My breath hitched. While that was sort of true, it wasn't exactly how it had played out. I guess Coach was trying to help me out. Sweet of her, but I'd have to set everyone straight. No more lying for me.

"I'm really sorry," I began. "First of all, I hope you all know that I would never, ever throw a game."

"Oh, we never believed that," Win scoffed. "Everyone

knew that was just Olive trying to stir things up."

I felt a wave of relief. Then, for the first time, I noticed that Olive wasn't there. "Um—where is she?" I asked.

"Suspended," Bianca informed me. She pursed her lips primly. "For cyberbullying."

"Lakeview has a zero-tolerance policy about that," Caroline added.

Behind me, the locker doors flew open again.

"Well, ladies, what are we waiting—" Coach broke off when she spotted me. "Park?" she said, frowning. "I'm confused."

I felt a flutter of doubt. "Um—I'm not suspended anymore," I explained. "Mr. Haverford said—"

"Not about that," Coach said impatiently. "I'm confused because we have less than fifteen minutes to warm up before the doors open, and you're not even changed yet. Hurry up and get into that uniform! The rest of you—warm-ups! Now!"

Everyone else filed obediently out of the locker room, but Helen lingered.

"You doing okay?" she asked.

"Yeah." I pulled my jersey over my head then faced her. "But you're being way nicer to me than I deserve. Do you want to know the truth?" I didn't wait for an answer. I didn't want to lose my nerve. "It wasn't Coach who asked to keep my public school past a secret. It was me. I lied to everyone. Including you."

"Oh, Pippa." Helen shook her head. "We played you in last year's season opener. It took me a bit to remember why you looked so familiar, but I've known you came from Victoria Middle since the week after you got here. I don't care."

I stared at her. "I don't get it. How come you didn't tell the Royals?"

Helen shrugged. "I figured that you had your own reasons for keeping it a secret. I was just waiting for you to come out with it on your own."

The locker door banged open. "Pelroy! Park!" Coach yelled. "Leave the therapy session for later! I want your butts on the court, now!"

Helen rolled her eyes at me, then jogged out the door. I took a deep breath and followed her. Game time.

. . .

Fifteen minutes later, the gym doors opened and hordes of spectators poured in. Within minutes, the bleachers were packed. The crowd noise was deafening as the clock counted down to the start of the game.

Along with me, the starting line-up included Helen, Win, Caroline, and Bianca. Although Bianca had stood up for me to Mr. Haverford, the cool, judgmental way she looked at me confirmed that it was more about my value to the team than anything else. Outside of this court, I doubted we would ever truly be friends. But tonight, we shared a common goal. I could live with that.

When the referee blew her whistle, the crowds quieted down and we jogged to the middle of the court. Helen approached the circle for the jump ball, and I found myself staring straight at Cami Villiger, my former teammate. She had gained two inches and fifteen pounds since last season, and looked fiercer than ever. She gave me a quick smile, which quickly transformed back into her game-face scowl. For the first time, I felt nerves stir in my stomach. There was a reason Victoria Middle had won this game for the last seven years. My old team was good. Really good.

I popped my knuckles, and my gaze briefly flickered up into the crowd. I scanned the rows for Jung-Hwa, needing a moment of reassurance. I spotted him in the exact middle of the bleachers. Next to him was someone I hadn't seen in at least a month. Buddy.

As I caught his eye, Buddy shot me a grin and a wave. I hadn't realized exactly how much I had missed him until that instant. Filled with happiness, I gave him a huge smile and an enthusiastic air five.

Buddy jumped up from his seat and Jung-Hwa went wild when he saw me.

"Gooooo Pippa!" he shouted, waving his hands over his head. Jung-Hwa had never been much of a sports person; I suppose he thought the gestures he was making were standard. But while a couple weeks ago I would have cringed, now I couldn't help but laugh.

Three rows away, Eliot's blond head drew my eye like a magnet. He was sitting with Matthew, and when they saw me, they both smiled. Eliot even gave a discreet wave.

Then the referee blew her whistle again, and it was time to focus on the game.

I took a deep breath and the tension drained out of my shoulders. For the first time in over a month, I felt that signature peace wash over me. This was my school. My court. My game. And I was ready to prove it.

The referee blew the whistle and we were off. Cami won the jump ball, automatically shooting down the court, and the rest of us followed, our legs pumping as hard as we could. Win cut Cami off, and Cami passed the ball to Victoria Middle's new small forward; I snatched it out of the girl's hands.

"Open!" Win called.

I passed it over. A perfect throw.

From there, the game sped forward, minute after minute ticking away on the time clock while I concentrated on the ball.

"Man-on-man, everyone," Coach Ahmed shouted. "Use those hips, Win!"

Victoria's shooting guard back-pedaled to the three-point line and made a perfect shot. Nothing but net. A loud whoop went up from the Victoria Middle side of the bleachers, and Cami made the swish signal toward the shooting guard, who grinned back.

3-0.

The referee blew his whistle, and Starsie jogged out-of-bounds. When the referee passed Starsie the ball and blew the whistle again, we all scrambled to get free.

"Over here," yelled Helen.

Starsie passed the ball over, and Helen shot down the court. Victoria Middle specialized in zone defense, rather than man-on-man, and as I sprinted toward one of the low blocks, Cami hurried over to guard me. For a brief second, our eyes met.

"Good luck, Park," she said.

"You, too," I responded.

"Pippa!" Helen called.

"Open!"

Helen pivoted on one foot and bounce-passed the ball

to me. I ducked in front of Cami, pushed her back with my butt, and turned around to sink a neat two-pointer. *Swish.* Yes. There it was. That intoxicating rush of adrenaline. Pure power.

"Nice shot, Park," Coach Ahmad called. "Now, defense, everybody!"

By the end of the first quarter I was running with sweat, and the score was 16-12, Victoria Middle. I had to give it to my old team: Their offense was killer. Victoria Middle's shooting guard had sunk another three-pointer already, and Cami had always been the best point guard around.

"Post up!" Coach Parr's command almost made me head for the basket, before I remembered that she now led my opponent's team.

Cami passed the ball to a girl named Anna, a muscular post, but I was on her so fiercely that she couldn't find the wiggle room to take a shot. She pivoted and took a faltering step back.

"Traveling!" The referee blew his whistle, and the ball was passed to our side.

Before play could resume, Coach Ahmad sent Kathy, Sam, and Venus onto the court; I retreated to the sidelines with Bianca and Helen.

"Short rest." Coach nodded at us.

I needed the break, but every second spent glued to

that bench felt agonizing; my leg bobbed up and down the entire time. When one of Victoria Middle's forwards made a layup nearly unguarded, I groaned, hating feeling helpless. Venus made up for it with an amazing two-pointer, but nothing could lessen my urge to be on the court again. Fortunately, it was just a few minutes before Coach put me back in.

By the final quarter, my legs felt like gelatin. Victoria Middle called a time out, and I gulped water down like it was air.

"You need another break, Park?" Coach asked.

I shook my head. "No, Coach." The words came out defensively, but there were less than two minutes left, and the game was neck and neck.

Coach chuckled. "All right, then." Raising her voice, she called, "Huddle up, team!"

We quickly formed a circle around her.

"The score is 30-31," she said. "We're only one point behind, girls. That's nothing. Keep your wits about you, and don't make stupid plays. We can win this, but only if we're in it together." Coach Ahmad glanced from face to face. "A minute and a half left," she said. "Don't waste it."

The whistle blew and we headed back onto the court.

It was our ball. Win passed it to Helen, who passed it to Bianca, who passed it to Caroline—who took a shot, only to watch it bounce off the rim. Cami lunged for the re-bound, but

I dove in between her and the ball, then tossed it over to Helen, who nailed a two-pointer.

"Lakeview takes the lead, 32-31," the referee said, making our side of the bleachers roar.

Gritting her teeth, Cami passed the ball to Anna, who barreled past Starsie.

"Defense, Park!" Coach yelled.

I scrambled into place as Anna dribbled closer, getting in position to steal the ball. But she was ready for me. She snarled, then made a fast break, sprinting forward past me, and past Helen, too. She made a perfect layup.

33-32.

One point behind again with—I glanced at the scoreboard and winced—thirty seconds to go. There was no time to catch my breath. Caroline passed the ball to Helen, who dribbled forward.

Bianca and I both sprinted down the court, hands up. Two Victoria players cornered Helen, who passed the ball to Bianca. But Bianca only managed two dribbles before Victoria's shooting guard trapped her. The girls stood chest-to-chest, with Bianca keeping the ball low to the ground as she looked for a way out.

Fifteen seconds left.

"Pippa!'" Bianca yelled, and threw the ball to me.

I caught it, but I'd barely cleared the three-point line

when Cami pressed in on me. She tried for another steal, and I fumbled the dribble and fell backward, scooping the ball to my chest.

If I took another step I'd get dinged for traveling. I glanced at the rim: I didn't know if I could make this shot.

Sweat dripped into my eyes. The clock showed five seconds left.

"Underdog! Underdog!" I heard a voice call out. Buddy's voice. *Everyone loves an underdog, Park!* His words came back to me—and suddenly, I wasn't in Lakeview's shiny gymnasium with two hundred people staring at me, with my old teammates smirking gleefully at each other. Instead, it was just Buddy and me, shooting hoops and exchanging stupid remarks on a scuffed-up basketball court in the park. *Every good player knows that the trick is to focus on your opponent's torso. Because eyes can lie, and so can shoulders, feet, and heads.*

These girls were good players . . . which was why I kept my shoulders straight forward up until the moment I passed the ball back to Bianca. I trusted her instincts and ability to catch the ball. She was captain for a reason.

There were two seconds left when she took her shot. I didn't have to look to know that it had gone in. Somehow, I felt it through my entire body.

When the buzzer went off, the score was 34-33. The crowd went wild.

Lakeview might have lost the last seven games, but number eight was ours.

27

GAME OVER

Inside the Petersen Sports Center, it was pure chaos.

The stands erupted into cheers while Coach Ahmad kissed the golden coin around her neck. Everyone on our team clung to each other, jumping and hugging at the same time, and Starsie squealed in my ear so loudly I thought my eardrum might burst. After sharing a high five with Helen, I turned to Bianca.

"Nice shot," I said.

"Thanks." She nodded at me with what might have been respect, and then went to hug Helen. I turned and found myself facing Eliot and Matthew.

"You put on a great show tonight," Matthew said, high-fiving me. "We were on the edge of our seats the whole game."

"Thanks! But what are you doing here?" I asked him. "I thought you'd be in military prison until you were forty."

He laughed. "Me too. But your act of insan—I mean, kindness—had a ripple effect. For once, my dad and I talked to each other instead of just yelling. And guess what? I got him to agree to let me audition for the conservatory. No matter what Aunt Evelyn threatens." He beamed. "You're my lucky charm, Pippa Park!" His gaze shifted to someone behind me. "Hey, Coach! What did I tell you about this kid?"

"I owe you one, Haverford." Coach Ahmad came up beside me and thumped me—hard—on the back. "I took a chance on the right player," she said. "Next year, we'll completely destroy them."

She and Matthew moved off a little ways, chatting. Eliot glanced toward them, but remained rooted in front of me, looking slightly lost. My body thrummed with so much residual adrenaline from the win that I could barely stop myself from hopping from foot to foot as I gazed at his glorious face. Even though I realized (with some surprise) that my monster crush on him had faded somewhat, I couldn't deny that he was utterly perfect-looking.

"Bianca sure nailed that last shot, didn't she?" I said.

Eliot cocked his head. "She did. But we wouldn't have won the game without your last pass. You played great."

My heart fluttered a teensy bit. *Stop it, Park.*

"Thanks," I said. "Anyways, I'll let you go. I'm sure Bianca's waiting for you."

Eliot shot me that mildly-baffled, mildly-annoyed look of his. "Why would Bianca be waiting for me?"

"Isn't she your girlfriend?"

Eliot's eyebrows pushed together. "Who told you that?"

Well, Bianca and Caroline certainly implied *it*, I thought. "Um, I just thought—I mean, I know you meet up with her sometimes and—"

"For *tutoring*," Eliot said, looking distinctly uncomfortable at the direction our conversation had taken. "She asked me for math help. Weren't you there for that?"

My mouth popped open. Just for tutoring? Nothing more?

Then Eliot said, "Anyway, she's a seventh grader. I don't date seventh graders."

For one moment, just one second, I felt utterly crushed. *Of course he doesn't date seventh graders*, I scolded myself. *What was I even thinking?*

Then, suddenly, I saw the humor in the situation. I started to laugh.

"What's so funny?" Eliot asked me suspiciously.

"Oh, nothing," I said. "Just happy. That's all. I'll see you around, Eliot."

"Tuesday, right?" he said.

"Tuesday!" I called over my shoulder as I walked away.

I pushed through the crowd in search of Jung-Hwa and Buddy. Finally, I spotted Buddy. To my surprise, he was standing with Helen and Win. I hurried up, but before I could do more than say hi, Win threw her arms around my shoulders.

"There wasn't time before the game, but I wanted to tell you that I felt so bad about what happened," she said. She lowered her voice and leaned in closer to whisper. "Also, you shouldn't be ashamed because your family owns a laundromat. My mom cleans houses, you know. I'm a scholarship student, too."

As I pulled back, blinking at Win in surprise, Helen clapped her hands.

"We need to celebrate this victory," she declared. "Together! There's no way I'm ready for this night to end."

Buddy nodded so hard I thought his neck would snap. "In my humble opinion, this is an occasion that calls for friendship, honor . . . and as much ice cream as we can possibly eat!"

Helen giggled. With a start, I noticed how close she was standing to Buddy—who, I noted, also had a distinctly pink tinge to his cheeks. My eyes widened in surprise. When Buddy glanced away, I waggled my eyebrows at Helen. She laughed.

"Well, should we all go to Duo's Diner?" Buddy suggested.

"Sounds good to me," Helen agreed.

"Hold that thought." I craned my neck, searching for Jung-Hwa. A moment later, I spotted him standing a few paces off. I ran over to him and whispered in his ear. He listened, then nodded, a big grin creeping over his face.

I turned to my friends. "I have a better idea," I declared. "Why don't we grab dinner at my place? Jung-Hwa will make the best kimchi-jjigae you've ever tasted, and the watermelon popsicles we have will blow your minds."

Tomorrow, I would start to deal with the remaining fallout from my poor grades and bad choices. But for now, as Jung-Hwa led the way to the door, and the rest of my friends followed, I laughed and joked along with them—and for the first time in the whole semester, I didn't feel like I was pretending.

I just felt like me: a little awkward, a little too enthusiastic, a little uncool. But a hundred percent Pippa Park.

PIPPA PARK
RAISES HER GAME

Bonus Content

Discussion Questions for Your Book Club

Q&A with Author Erin Yun

Glossary of Korean Words

Discussion Questions for Your Book Club

1. Pippa isn't an orphan, but at times she feels like one. Describe Pippa's relationship with Mina, her older sister. Why is Mina so tough on Pippa? Discuss whether Mina resents taking care of Pippa. How is Jung-Hwa, Mina's husband, a father figure to Pippa? How does he make Pippa feel better after she has a fight with Mina?

2. What is the definition of family? Explain why Pippa's mother had to return to Korea. How are Mina and Jung-Hwa realizing the American dream? Discuss how Pippa's family situation is similar to that of new Americans throughout our nation. How are many of them separated from their loved ones? Discuss why it's important to celebrate all types of families.

3. Pippa says, "At Lakeview I could be anyone, as long as they didn't find out the truth about me." What doesn't she want the kids at Lakeview to know about her? What does she do to keep her home life private? What does Pippa think would happen if the girls found out the truth about her?

4. How does trying to fit in cause Pippa to lose her sense of self? Why is she ashamed of her family and the way they live? At the end of the novel, Pippa invites the basketball team to her apartment. What is significant about this gesture?

5. Pippa's best friend at Victoria Middle is Buddy Johnson. Think about how she betrays him. Discuss the apology and explanation for her behavior that she might give to Buddy.

6. Why does Pippa think that Eliot's family life is more messed up than hers? How does knowing about his family make her better understand Eliot? At what point does Mr. Haverford gain the courage to stand up to Aunt Evelyn?

7. Olive Giordano is the student ambassador that shows Pippa around the school. How does Olive's desire to be popular affect her judgment and turn her into a cyber-bully? When Pippa learns that Olive is Throwaway, how does that make Pippa feel? Discuss cyberbullying in your school.

8. Discuss what Jung-Hwa means when he says, "The lower you fall, the more room you have to rise." What is Pippa's lowest point? How do you know that she is about to rise? Have you ever felt the same way?

9. Pippa's family celebrates Chuseok: Korean Thanksgiving Day. Learn more about the traditions associated with this holiday on the Internet. Describe and discuss the holiday and the food that is prepared. What cultural holidays does your family celebrate? Is there anything special that you eat?

10. *Pippa Park Raises Her Game* is a contemporary reimagining of *Great Expectations*. Use books or the Internet to find out about the main characters in *Great Expectations*. What is each character's counterpart in *Pippa Park Raises Her Game*? List the characters, side by side and as a group apply two or three adjectives that best describe each of them.

11. Think about all that has happened to Pippa. Then consider the following quote from *Great Expectations*: "And it was not until I began to think, that I began fully to know how wrecked I was, and how the ship in which I had sailed was gone to pieces." What is the metaphorical ship that Pippa sails? At what point does Pippa realize "how wrecked" her life is? How does she turn her life around once she begins "thinking"?

12. If you were to pick one character from *Pippa Park Raises Her Game* who is most like you, who would it be and why? Who is most unlike you and why? Which character from the book would you want as your friend and why?

FUN FACTS ABOUT ERIN YUN

1. She's obsessed with personality quizzes and takes them for her characters.

2. She is half Korean, and half Polish/Germanic.

3. Her favorite foods include: kimchi-jjigae, cherry ice cream, and walnut cakes filled with red bean.

4. She ran a bubblegum-selling business in middle school until it was shut down.

5. Her family lore says that her grandfather lost part of his farm in a game of Go-Stop.

6. She likes creating scavenger hunts in which participants dress like secret agents and follow clues.

7. Her favorite places in the world include Seoul, London, and Tokyo.

8. She was president of the New York University policy debate team.

9. Her family dogs, Belle and Yoko, both bark incredibly loudly despite being foolishly tiny.

10. She lives in New York City, but folks can tell she grew up in Texas by how often she says *ya'll*.

Q & A with Author Erin Yun

Did you draw from your own experiences when you wrote *Pippa Park Raises Her Game*?
My mom is Korean, and my dad is a mix of Polish and Germanic. In the book, the protagonist is a Korean American girl, and a lot of her favorite things—from her love of walnut cakes filled with red bean to the Korean drama *Boys Over Flowers*—were my favorite things growing up as well. The Chuseok scene where Pippa is playing the card game Go-Stop was also inspired by the time when my Mom casually mentioned that my grandfather had lost a farm during a high-stakes game . . . I'm not sure if this is true or if it was an intimidation tactic of hers—my brother and I always lost our allowance money to my Mom's Go-Stop prowess.

How did you come up with the characters?
One of the most fun things about drafting the book was deciding which characters from *Great Expectations* would become which characters in *Pippa Park Raises Her Game*, and how the updated characters would diverge from the originals. Some of the first characters that made it into the book (besides Pip/Pippa, of course!) were Biddy (now Buddy), Joe (now Jung-Hwa), and Estella (now Eliot).

Who is your favorite character in the book?
I guess this question depends on the definition of favorite. Since the book is written in first person, I spent so much time in Pippa's mind that I can't help but be a little partial

toward her even if I'm also the most critical of her at times. But I also have a soft spot for Jung-Hwa since he is such a sweetheart and a father figure to Pippa.

Tell us more about the process of creating Pippa Park's character.
Even before I started writing the book, I was already brainstorming Pippa's character. I would draw sketches of her, make playlists of songs I think she would listen to, and take personality quizzes for her. (She's an ESFP in case anyone was wondering.) I would also just daydream random conversations where she was talking to her friends or Mina or her teachers—anything that could let me get a feel for her voice.

Does she remind you of yourself at all?
Hmm, in some ways, yes. We both burst into tears during arguments, are terrible at math, and adore walnut cakes, for example. But I think we're quite different, as well. Pippa is more exuberant and bolder than I am, while I'm a little more introverted and dreamier than she is. Plus, she's much better at basketball. Like, way better.

What inspired the key family relationship and dynamic between Jung-Hwa, Mina, and Pippa?
Jung-Hwa's relationship with Mina is based on many different inspirations: the relationship between Joe Gargery and Mrs. Gargery from *Great Expectations*, of course, but also the relationship between Jan-di's parents from one of my favorite Korean dramas growing up—*Boys Over Flowers*—

with a touch of the dynamic between my own parents. As a kid, I always knew that the general rule was that if I wanted something big, like a new phone, my mom would be the most likely to say yes, but if I wanted something small, like a magazine or some ice cream, my dad was the person to go to.

Why did you become a writer?
There wasn't a particular reason; it's just something I've always done and always loved. I've been writing for longer than I can remember—first, in old notebooks with such terrible handwriting that no one, not even myself, would ever be able to decipher it, and then later, on the family computer whenever I could fight off my siblings for computer time.

When you're having trouble writing, what do you usually do?
I like to listen to music and kind of just zone out. Once my mind relaxes, I can start to hear the conversations of the various characters hanging around my mind. It's often not the scene I'm working on. Sometimes, it's not even the characters I'm writing. But it helps to give me a creativity boost and a fresh perspective, and it lets me go back to the text feeling reenergized.

What do you like to do when you aren't writing?
I like debating, traveling (favorite places include Seoul, South Korea, and London, England), and playing games—I'm terrible at *Mario Kart* but unwisely competitive about it.

Korean Language Glossary and Pronunciation Guide

Chuseok 추석 (choo-suk) *noun:* an autumn harvest moon festival celebrated on the full moon on the fifteenth day of the eight month according to the lunar calendar; falls in late September or early October

gangaji 강아지 (gahng-ah-jee) *noun:* a puppy or dog

gochujang 고추장 (go-chew-jjahng) *noun:* a spicy, fermented red chili paste used in many Korean dishes such as bibimbap and tteokbokki

jahp-chae 잡채 (jahp-chae) *noun:* potato starch (glass) noodles and assorted vegetables sliced Julienne-style and seasoned with soy sauce and sesame oil; often served as a side dish on special occasions such as Chuseok

kimchi 김치 (ghim-chee) *noun:* spicy, fermented Napa cabbage served with all Korean meals; the national dish of South Korea

kimchi-jjigae 김치찌개 (ghim-chee-jee-gae) *noun:* a spicy kimchi-based stew made with a variety of ingredients such as scallions, onions, tofu, pork, or seafood

Omma (Eomma) 엄마 (uhm-ma) *noun:* mom or mommy

tteokbokki 떡볶이 (duck-boke-ee) *noun:* a spicy stir-fried snack made with chewy cylindrical rice cakes and gochujang; eaten as a common street food

saranghae 사랑해 (sah-rahng-hae) *phrase:* I love you (informal)

yeobo 여보 (yuh-bo) *noun:* a term of endearment for one's spouse

yeot 엿 (yuht) *noun:* a variety of sticky, sugary traditional Korean confectionary often resembling taffy or candy

---

Romanization source:
http://roman.cs.pusan.ac.kr/input_eng.aspx

Acknowledgments

I am so thankful for so many people who helped make *Pippa Park Raises Her Game* what it is. While I don't have time to give a shout-out to each individual, please know how much I appreciate you all.

First, my endless appreciation and love to Tracey. You put in infinite amounts of work to help make *Pippa Park Raises Her Game* the best version of the book it could be, including giving me amazing feedback, helping me whenever I came across plot holes or other complications, and inspiring me with some of the best pep talks in the world. Not to mention all of the snacks you gave me! To Kate, Susan, Eloise, Liz, and Ellen—you turned *Pippa* from a very messy draft to something I truly love, and hope others will love too. I am so grateful for your wisdom, time, and talent. And for your patience when dealing with extremely messy timelines. My endless appreciation to the rest of the Fabled Team as well, including Nicole, Stacey, and Sam. Ya'll are magic, and I love working with you all. Also, special thanks to Bev Johnson, our wonderful illustrator. When I first saw your rendition of Pippa on the cover of the book, I nearly cried. You do such beautiful work! And, of course, a massive thank you to everyone else behind the pages who helped make this book a reality, including Debra, Gillian, Jaime, and Pat. I couldn't have done it without all of you!

Next, my forever love and gratitude to my family. Mom and

Dad, thank you for always believing in me and lifting me up when I am down. Without your endless amounts of support, I wouldn't exist, much less this book. Thank you also to the world's best siblings, Natalie and Daniel. You never fail to inspire, challenge, and amaze me. And a family shout-out can't exist without mentioning my dogs, Belle and Yoko. Yoko, you might have won the award for Most Distracting Dog, but it was your endless barking that encouraged me to take writing breaks every once in a while, so maybe you were just looking out for me.

Thank you to all my friends—your support, enthusiasm, and appreciation for my writing truly touches my heart. Yasaswi Pisupati and Jenny Duo Zheng, I promised both of you that when my book was published, I would mention you in my acknowledgments page, so here we are. It's only fair since you two deserve all the book acknowledgments. And Alex, thank you for everything you do for me, and for everything you did for this book. You were my go-to person whenever I was conflicted about something, answered dozens of hypothetical plot and character questions, and didn't complain when I texted you questions at 2 a.m., like "Which of these names sounds the most pleasing?" Your enthusiasm and support for Pippa always makes me blush. I love you.

And finally, thank you to all the readers who picked up this book. It means the world to me, and although you can't hear me right now, I am actually screaming. You are amazing.

About the Author

Erin Yun grew up in Frisco, Texas and used to play basketball as a middle grader. She received her BFA in English from New York University and is currently pursuing her Masters in Creative Writing at the University of Cambridge. Erin is a member of the Society of Children's Book Writers and Illustrators and has written reviews and articles for BookBrowse. She developed the Pippa Park Author Program, an interactive writing workshop, which she has conducted in person and virtually at schools, libraries, and bookstores. This is her first children's book.

About Fabled Films & Fabled Films Press

Fabled Films is a publishing and entertainment company creating original content for young readers and middle-grade audiences. Fabled Films Press combines strong literary properties with high quality production values to connect books with generations of parents and their children. Each property is supported by websites, educator guides and activities for bookstores, educators, and librarians, as well as videos, social media content and supplemental entertainment for additional platforms.

FABLED FILMS PRESS
NEW YORK CITY
fabledfilms.com

Connect with Fabled Films and *Pippa Park Raises Her Game*:
www.pippapark.com
www.fabledfilms.com
Facebook: @Fabled.Films.Press | Instagram: @fabled.films
Twitter: @fabled_films

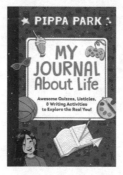